RYANN FLETCHER

Bearfaced Lie

Midwest Weres book 4

Cover art by Indy Art & Illustration

https://www.instagram.com/strooooble/

First edition

ISBN: 978-1-7393585-3-2

This book was professionally typeset on Reedsy.
Find out more at reedsy.com

To everyone who yearns for the sun: it's always darkest before the dawn, the winter solstice, and the last hour of your shift.
Light is coming.
So is your next chapter.

Contents

Chapter One

The cans were all lined up in neat, perfect columns, the labels facing forward in unison. Chicken soup on the left, cream of mushroom on the right, and there were still twelve aisles to go. Leah sighed, in spite of herself and the reprimand she'd get from management if she didn't pick up the pace soon. She'd already gotten snide comments about how she was the slowest in the department, and no one would let her swap to overnights. She'd prefer to be left alone to do her work, not be interrupted by rude customers whenever she finally found something resembling a groove in which she could reliably complete her tasks.

The watch on her wrist flashed a glare from the harsh overhead fluorescent lights that danced against the paper labels, emblazoned with the company's minimalistic logo. Three and a half hours to go until she could leave, until she could go back to her apartment, eat two packs of cheap noodles, and pass out in front of the television until her alarm went off the following morning. Two hundred and ten minutes left, twelve thousand, six hundred seconds. If she could only focus on her work, and not the painful, mind-numbing boredom, she might just manage to avoid getting fired right before Christmas.

"Hey there, Erickson," her coworker said, leaning against the end cap. She was picking at an opened package of ribbon, the curls spilling out over the sides of the shelf. "I didn't see your name on the schedule today."

Leah slid another can onto the shelf, tin scraping against steel with an unpleasant screech. "Hey, Jasmine," she mumbled. "Picked up a shift for Greg, that's all."

"I'm surprised anyone would come in voluntarily, especially recently," Jasmine said, tightening the long, brunette ponytail that swished over her shoulders when she walked. "When do you clock out?"

"Not soon enough."

"I hear that—I only just got here. Closing shift tonight, I can't *wait*." Jasmine's tone dripped with sarcasm as she nudged the corner of the plastic crate with the toe of her scuffed shoe. "Looks like they have you on stocking duty."

Leah nodded. "Yep. As usual." One more can and the shelf was done, and she shifted to the next, this one filled with beans and fish. She wiped her hands on her grey apron, unsure of where the sticky residue had come from, and unwilling to investigate. "It's not like anyone else wants to be back here doing this, not with the new guidelines sent down from corporate."

"Everything must be properly faced and organized," Jasmine parroted in a mocking tone. "Hilarious that they think that's even possible on a skeleton crew in December."

"Did you see the gift wrap aisle?" Leah asked. "It looks like a craft store threw up." She nodded at the ribbon on the end cap as she stacked three more tins of tuna on top of each other, pulling them to the front of the shelf. "There's plenty more where that came from. I'm dreading even going over there."

"I'd help, but I'm on cash," Jasmine replied, apologetic. "And you know how they feel about people on cash wandering away from the line. Heaven forbid someone has to wait longer than ten seconds to check out." She unlocked her phone, frowning at it. "Shit, I have to go. I'm supposed to be at the register in about ninety seconds."

Leah glanced at her before returning to picking an old, expired label off the shelf. It looked like it had been there for at least six months. "Better hurry," she offered. "No more grace periods on being late, remember. You'll get docked fifteen minutes no matter what."

"I know, I'm going, I'm going," Jasmine tossed over her shoulder, disappearing into the next aisle. "Hey, Leah, they put the new schedule out," she called over the tall shelves. "In case you were waiting to see if you got the holidays off or not."

Leah stiffened, hovering over a bag of dried lentils that belonged on the opposite side. "Uh, great, thanks, I'll check it out when I'm off the clock."

Jasmine was visible once more, walking backwards towards the front of the store. "Any plans?"

"None worth getting out of bed for," Leah replied, but in a voice she knew wasn't loud enough to carry across the store.

There was no reply, probably because Jasmine was already running for the front. Leah could hear the squeak of her shoes against the freshly waxed tile floor. Already, the monthly fear of the schedule was resting uncomfortably in her bones, waiting to pounce the way it always did, every twenty nine days.

More shelves stacked as the crate at her feet emptied of its stock while Leah worked up one aisle and down the next, collecting the random items left where they didn't go. Reaching behind a line of generic Syndicorp-branded cookies, she pulled out warm lunch meat, swallowing back a retch. It must have been there for days, just lying in wait for her to find it. She didn't blame people for deciding not to purchase something, but it wasn't the first time she'd discovered spoiled food, and it certainly wouldn't be the last.

Near the third end cap, Leah straightened, bracing a hand against her back as she stood. Her muscles were cramped and exhausted from hours of crouching near to the ground, and she'd pay the price for it later with a heating pad and plenty of painkillers to dull the incessant, insistent throbbing ache at the base of her spine.

It was snowing lightly outside, a fine mist of heavy snow that had already begun to collect on the asphalt, blurring the yellow painted lines that separated the parking spaces. One more winter in Rockland Heights probably wouldn't kill her, but she was starting to wonder how much damage it had already done. She was twenty-nine with a master's degree, and nothing to show for it other than a crappy rented apartment and a car that was almost old enough to legally drink in some counties.

Wherever she should have been, it wasn't Rockland Heights. Once a place full of promise, the factories had closed, sending jobs overseas. The small businesses had been ousted by Syndicorp, the same people who signed her meager paychecks. All that was left was a derelict town center in desperate need of investment no one wanted to provide.

Leah pushed through the swinging door into the back room, heaving out a sigh of relief. One more shift down, thousands to go before she had enough saved up to leave town for good. People weren't meant to stick around where they were raised, or at least, she wasn't. Her heart thudded in her chest as she flipped the first page of the schedule clipboard over, and then it dropped heavily into her stomach when she saw *Leah Erickson* scheduled right across the full moon just after Christmas.

She was sure she'd requested it off, not that it meant anything to management. Drawing in a deep breath, her hands shaking, she knocked on the closed door at the edge of the back room. "Ma'am?" she called softly through the reinforced steel. "Mrs. Campbell?" she tried again, when there was no answer.

"Come in," came the gruff, frustrated reply.

The hinges squealed in protest, and Leah clasped her hands in front of her. "Mrs. Campbell, I'm afraid there's been a mistake," she said softly. "I'm sure I requested the two days after Christmas off, but I just saw myself on the schedule."

"Them's the breaks," Mrs. Campbell said, without even looking away from her computer. She was playing solitaire in one window, and refreshing the work email address in another. "You've been here long enough to know that requests at the holidays can't always be honored."

"I requested these days six months ago," Leah protested gently. "As soon as we could even put in requests for the holidays. I even worked Thanksgiving night and the day after."

Mrs. Campbell yawned, adjusting the collar of her ill-fitting blazer, her name tag askew across the pocket. "Two higher up than you put in their requests last week," she replied. "I can't help seniority."

"But I can't work then!" Leah refuted, louder this time, and it was enough to drag her manager's eyes from the screen.

"Then you will have to find someone to cover your shift."

Leah swallowed back an angry growl that purred low in her throat. "No one is going to want to work those days for me, not right after Christmas. This whole town empties out because everyone would rather be somewhere else."

"You are more than welcome to find someone to cover your shift." Mrs. Campbell opened a new window, typing into the box one finger at a time. "I've made a note of this, so if you decide to call out on those days, we will know what happened, and it will count triple against your allowable missed shifts." She turned, offering Leah a serpentine smile. "Was there anything else?"

"No."

"Excellent. Please close the door on your way out, I'm in the middle of something important." Mrs. Campbell turned back to her computer, pulling up the tab with solitaire once again. "You might try asking the new hire to take your shifts, she seems hungry for them." She flicked at a roster hanging on the wall, running her finger down the list until she located the correct name. "Jasmine Reed. Did you need her number?"

"Er—" Leah tried, but got cut off by the phone ringing noisily on the desk.

"Try her," Mrs. Campbell said, picking up the receiver and shooing Leah out the door with the sharp flick of her wrist. "Hello, Steve, how wonderful to hear from you! Yes, of course we got the new commerce targets—no, unfortunately not, but—"

Leah backed out of the office before she had to listen to another word from the corporate office about how their store was chronically under-target compared to the rest in their district. According to higher-ups at headquarters four states away, there was no excuse for not having consistent growth, not even a town where most people were barely making rent. Most folks just bought what they needed, and nothing more—and the neighboring town housed plenty of people with money, but enough money that shopping at Syndicorp wasn't going to be their first choice.

She stared at the schedule again, blood pounding in her ears. There was no point in asking the new girl to take her shifts, she looked like a nice, normal person who probably had a nice family to spend the holidays with. There was no way she would ever consider giving that up for someone she barely knew and had barely spoken to, and never outside of work.

Leah hissed out a sigh, smacking the clipboard as it dropped back against the wall with a noisy clack, the attached pen dangling from a dirty length of twine that had been there for at least eighteen months, ever since she'd started at Syndicorp. It was supposed to be for a couple of months, but she'd gotten stuck in the cycle of it, just like she'd been afraid she would.

She couldn't work those days, she'd look like she had the flu and feel even worse. If she wasn't careful, she'd wind up in the hospital over it, and that wouldn't be the first time. Leah allowed a small grumble to resonate in her throat, dampened by her tongue.

Reaching for the phone on the desk, she rifled through the file, calling the first person on the list who had indicated they wanted more shifts. "Hi, is that Greg?" she asked. "Yeah, I was hoping you could take a few shifts for me from the twenty-sixth until the—yeah, yeah, of course, I understand." She hung up, glaring at the page.

She called four more with the same results. Six people had requested off, and three had been granted the request. Leah leaned forward, resting her forehead against the counter. Jasmine Reed was the only one left to ask.

Chapter Two

Beep. Beep. Beep. Jasmine scanned each item across the red flashing light, packaging crunching noisily as she located the barcodes. She worked quickly and efficiently, packing the groceries as she worked. "That's forty-two seventeen," she announced, beaming across the counter.

"Hang on, I have to write a check," the man said, fumbling in the inside breast pocket of his parka.

"No problem," Jasmine replied, trying her best to plaster a smile across her face, knowing the transaction would net her a bad score on her timing. From the corner of her eye, the screen flashed yellow, and then red as the man slowly wrote out the numbers.

"Who do I make it out to?" he asked, pen poised over the paper.

Jasmine swallowed back an irritated sigh. "Syndicorp, just like on the front of the store!" she said brightly.

"Oh, hang on, I wrote the wrong amount," the man said, scribbling over the ruined check and starting another.

The line began to lengthen, and the customers were already four-deep. The woman behind him cleared her throat noisily, glaring at Jasmine as if she could make the man write any faster.

"Is this the only checkout?" the woman asked, glancing around.

Jasmine nodded. "I'm afraid so, ma'am. Just me tonight!"

"You could stand to work a little faster, people have things to do." The woman turned to the next in line behind her, talking behind her hand as though it muffled what she said, when it unequivocally did not. "I swear, I always get the cashiers who spend more time talking than scanning."

"Here you go!" the man said triumphantly, handing over the check. Jasmine glanced at his driver's license and slid the paper into the cash drawer as she handed him his receipt.

"Thank you for shopping with us!" she said, already turning to scan the next items on the belt. Beep. Beep.

"The barcode is missing on this, I'll have to call someone," Jasmine said, reaching for the phone that controlled the speaker system.

The woman rolled her eyes, smacking her ring of keys against the counter. "Are you kidding me?"

"I'm afraid not, ma'am, there's no barcode on this soap." Jasmine picked up the phone, speaking into it with a polite, even tone. "Associates, cash desk three needs a price check, thank you!" She hung up, continuing to scan the remaining items. To her mounting horror, no one had appeared by the time she finished. "I'll run back and grab one myself," she told the woman, easing out from behind the register. "I'll only be a minute."

"I've got it," Leah said, handing over a fresh box with the code intact.

"Nice one, Erickson," Jasmine said, already relieved. "I thought you were off already."

"I am, just thought I'd help. I think there's only one person out on the floor." Leah hesitated, leaning against the counter for a moment before helping the woman pack up the rest of her groceries. "Have a good night," she said, zipping up her navy blue parka, the faux fur in the hood waving in the artificial heating from the vent overhead.

"Yeah, you too." Jasmine handed over the customer's receipt and began on the next transaction, desperate for the line to thin.

"I'll grab a code sheet for you from the back," Leah offered. "Has almost every SKU in there, helps when the barcodes come off."

"You don't have to do that," Jasmine said, preparing the screen for a new transaction. "Anyway, you're already off the clock! Go home, put your feet up!"

"Nah, I know where they are," Leah said. "I'll only be a minute."

The next customer was an older lady, prim and proper in her perfectly matching outerwear, the forest green peacoat the same hue as her wool beret. "Good evening, ma'am, I hope you found everything you were looking for today?"

"How come the price of orange juice has gone up so much?" the lady demanded. "Just last week it was two fifty, this week it's two seventy-five!"

Jasmine nodded, continuing to scan. "I'm not sure, ma'am, we don't set prices at the store level. That's all corporate. I can give you a survey code if you—"

"No, no, I don't want any damned survey," the lady said. "I want to know why you're trying to bankrupt me!"

"Oh, uh, as I said, we don't have any control—"

The lady dropped her bags into the cart with noisy clatters indicative of her frustration. "Nonsense. You have that computer there, you could change the price if you wanted to. Now I saw this same orange juice at the store in the next town for twenty-five cents cheaper. You should do a price match if you want to stay in business."

"Unfortunately ma'am, I don't have the authority to—"

"I want to speak to a manager!"

Jasmine reached for the phone again, closing her eyes so the lady wouldn't see her rolling them up to the ceiling. "Mrs. Campbell to cash desk three please, Mrs. Campbell to cash desk three." She laid the phone back in its holder, smiling over the counter. "I'm sure it will just be a moment."

"This is outrageous, you know, fleecing people right before Christmas." The lady tapped her debit card against the cart's handle, an irritating rhythm that didn't match with the canned, instrumental covers of carols overhead. "You should be ashamed of yourself."

Mrs. Campbell approached, somehow simultaneously shooting daggers at Jasmine while beaming happily at the customer. "What's the problem here?" she asked, stepping behind the register.

"This lady would like a price match on the orange juice," Jasmine offered. "Twenty-five cent difference."

"Of course, of course," Mrs. Campbell said, sliding her lanyard over the register to authorize the override. "That's all done for you, ma'am."

"See?" the lady said, jabbing her finger at Jasmine. "I told you that you could help if you really wanted to." She wheeled her cart out of the lane and out the door into the polite snow that blew across the windows.

"This line is getting out of control," Mrs. Campbell hissed into Jasmine's ear. "Given your last score, I'm not surprised. Pick up the pace, Jasmine. I was told you could keep up here, but so far it doesn't seem like it."

Anger flared beneath Jasmine's skin, but she ignored it, letting the embers die back into a quiet, destructive rage that was probably already giving her an ulcer. "The last transaction was a customer with a check," she countered, doing her best to defend herself. "He had to start over twice."

"That's no excuse for poor service," Mrs. Campbell retorted. "Get those speed scores up, or we'll have to have you in for unpaid remedial training if you want to keep your position here at Syndicorp." She smiled at the next person in line, handing over a stack of coupons. "I'm so sorry for the wait, she's new and having some trouble learning the ropes."

Jasmine reached for the next product on the belt, a large flat of water. "I'm not having—"

"And don't forget, you should be asking each and every guest—not customer, guest—if they want to sign up for our store card. Remember, you're supposed to be getting four sign-ups each shift, and so far I haven't seen a single one from you."

"Understood," Jasmine said through gritted teeth, straining from the weight of the water as she lifted it, the awkward height pulling a muscle in her back. She knew she'd pay for it later. "Thank you." She completed the transaction with a smile, letting the quiet injustice consume her from the inside out. Jasmine leaned against the counter, rubbing her lower back and already dreaming of the hot shower she'd take when she got home.

"Here's that scan sheet," Leah said, reappearing. It was laminated and secured with a split ring through punched holes at the top of each page. "All the usual ones are on the first page, and then it's alphabetical."

"Maybe it will keep me from getting fired," Jasmine said, sliding the scan sheet into her drawer. "Just what we all need around the holidays, being single *and* unemployed."

Leah shifted nervously, playing with the zipper of her coat, sliding it up and down the plastic teeth. "I know what you mean," she said. "Family doesn't really understand."

"You didn't answer me before, you know," Jasmine said, wiping down the conveyor belt with a harsh-smelling cleaning agent. "If you had plans for Christmas or not."

"Oh, uh..." Leah trailed off, her gaze affixed to the outside. "Not really. Family lives out on the coast. It's just me here."

"You don't want to go and see them?"

Leah shrugged. "I have to work." She grabbed two candy bars and put them on the belt, nodding to Jasmine. "And maybe between you and me, they aren't really worth the trip."

"Sounds like my dad's side," Jasmine offered, knowing all too well how destructive family could be. "But I'll be at my mom's this year, just like every year." She glanced up at Leah before scanning both of the sweets and taking the money, the exact cash amount. Her till flashed green, and her score bumped up just a couple of percentage points. "I live there with her and my grandpa." She nodded towards the screen. "Thanks for getting me out of the dog house."

"We've all gotta watch out for each other," Leah said. "It's not like Syndicorp is going to lift a finger for us." She opened one of the candy bars, taking a large bite from one side, the caramel trailing long and loopy before snapping. "Besides, I was starving. Forgot to bring lunch."

"You should have asked, I'd share. My mom packed me way too much in the way of leftovers. I swear, I'll be eating baked ziti for the rest of my life." Jasmine slid out from behind the register to rearrange the candy bars, keenly aware of the security cameras watching her every move. She'd definitely get fired if Mrs. Campbell caught her doing anything other than relentlessly working, even after the line was cleared.

"Uh, I did have a favor to ask, actually," Leah said between bites.

Jasmine raised an eyebrow, bending to scrape a sticker off the floor. "Shoot," she said.

"It's fine if you can't do it, I get that people are busy this time of year, and you don't really know me besides that, and it's probably a huge imposition to—"

"Out with it, Erickson," Jasmine encouraged, frowning as she flicked the dirty paper into the small trash bin under her counter. "Unless you're asking for a kidney. I can't give you one, because I only have one."

"What?" Leah said. "Uh, no, it's just, I..."

"Relax, I'm joking," Jasmine said. "Not about the kidney thing though, I really do only have one. Gave the other to my brother about ten years ago."

"Oh," Leah said softly.

"He's usually appreciative when he's not being extremely irritating." Jasmine snorted a small laugh. "But he's usually being extremely irritating. Still, he's my brother, even if he did run off to the West Coast to chase his dreams of being a pro surfer." She moved to the next cash register, cleaning that one too. "What's the favor?"

"I need a few shifts covered," Leah said. "They're right after Christmas, though, and you said you were going home to your family, so—"

"When?"

"The twenty-sixth and twenty-seventh," Leah said sheepishly. "Don't worry about it actually, forget I asked." She turned to walk away when a sparkling, brilliant plan hatched in Jasmine's head.

"Wait," she said. "Are you opposed to making a deal? A trade?"

"What kind of trade?"

Jasmine scrubbed at a discoloration on the conveyor belt, wondering what had caused it, and then deciding she probably didn't want to know. "My family, I love them, but they can be a bit... overbearing, around the holidays."

"I feel like that's probably pretty common," Leah offered, pocketing the empty wrapper and pulling on a pair of thick mittens. "It's why so many people dread going home."

"They worry about me," Jasmine said. "It started with the kidney thing, I had some complications. I'm fine now, but you know how it is." She picked up a discarded box of oatmeal, setting it into the bin underneath to have it re-shelved. "My mom and grandpa have been on me to start dating again. Pretty bad breakup a few years ago." Jasmine straightened, wincing at the pain in her back. "Pretend to be my date for Christmas, and I'll take those shifts for you."

Leah laughed, hiding her face with a cabled mitten. "Okay, okay, I'll ask someone else," she said.

"I'm serious." Jasmine squirted the belt again with the cleaner, washing it for the second time. "They worry too much, and if they thought I was dating again, maybe they'd sleep better." She shrugged. "Free dinner and you wouldn't have to spend Christmas alone."

"I always spend Christmas alone," Leah said, and then shook her head. "Sorry, I didn't mean to say it like that. I just mean that it's no bother to be by myself. I treat myself to some really good authentic Chinese food from the place under my apartment and watch television all day."

"Am I that repulsive that you'd rather work these shifts than spend a day with my family?" Jasmine asked, an eyebrow raised. "What do you need the time off for, anyway?"

"Just kind of a monthly ritual," Leah answered. "I find it hard to deal."

Jasmine nodded. "Oh. Yeah, I hear you. It can be rough sometimes." She set the spray bottle down to tighten the strings of her apron. "So what do you say, Leah? Do we have a deal?"

Leah jammed her hands into her pockets, avoiding eye contact as she considered her options. "Yeah, alright," she said finally. Deal."

Chapter Three

Briefly, Leah wondered what was worse: spending the holidays with a stranger's family and having to pretend she didn't want to crawl out the nearest window, or shifting into her grizzly self while working a night shift. In her estimation, it was a pretty equal competition, which is why she'd been sitting in the parking lot of the Jazzy Java cafe, a few towns over from where she lived. Jasmine said it would be best, so that no one would hear their plotting.

Leah's hand stayed on the keys in the ignition, strongly considering turning the engine over and driving away. She'd have to face Jasmine at work, of course, unless she faked her own death and moved to another state. She sighed. If there was anything she didn't have money for, it was a deposit on a new apartment just to avoid an awkward situation.

Throwing out a loud, private, aggrieved sigh, she pocketed the keyring and climbed out of the car, nearly falling over when her worn boot hit the ice. Cursing under her breath, she straightened, clicking the fob to lock the car and regain some crumbs of dignity.

The cafe was warm and inviting, with festive music being piped in over the speakers, and a candy cane garland strung across the edge of the counter.

"Hello!" the barista chirped. "What can I get for you today?" She was young, no older than sixteen, her round cheeks creased into a surprisingly genuine smile. Her name tag read Dee, adorned with a sketch of a reindeer.

"Uh, I don't know, what's good here?" Leah asked, looking around for Jasmine. So far, she hadn't arrived.

"My personal favorite is the hot chocolate with two pumps of peppermint," Dee said. "Three, if you're feeling brave or really want to feel like you're being walloped by a burlap sack full of festive feeling."

"Just the two," Leah said. "And maybe that muffin." She pointed at the glass case, a huge lemon poppyseed ripe for the eating. She shrugged. "Please."

"Of course, coming right up! Just me on shift for the moment, so give me a second to get you all sorted." The barista disappeared behind the counter, crouching down for something, rummaging around in a cardboard box. "Sorry, I ran out of cup sleeves." She resurfaced, branded sleeves in hand, red and green for the occasion. "Mara likes to really go all out this time of year."

"Yeah, I can tell." Leah ran a hand through her hair, irritated that it was already too long. She could have sworn it was only a week ago that she had gotten it cut, but it was falling into her eyes, dragging across her collar. No one in Rockland Heights ever wanted to cut her hair the way she wanted, short and shaved at the sides, because they all warned her it wouldn't be flattering, as if Leah cared about that. Who was she trying to impress, anyway?

"You came!" Jasmine said, pushing through the door. Her long, jade-green parka was unzipped, flapping around her hips. "I wasn't sure you would."

"I need those shifts covered, and you didn't give me much of a choice," Leah replied. "Besides, it's nice to get out of town for a day, even if it's only fifteen miles up the road."

Jasmine leaned against the counter on her forearms, squinting at the menu on the far wall. "So what did you get?"

"Peppermint hot chocolate."

"Two pumps, or three?" Jasmine asked.

Leah shrugged. "Two."

"Coward." Jasmine pulled a punch card out of her wallet, sliding it across the counter. "I've got this one. They love me here, and not just because my name matches the sign outside."

"No, you don't have to do that," Leah protested. "We make the same hourly, and—"

"I'm two punches away from a free drink, Erickson," Jasmine argued. "Just let me have this." She moved to the glass counter, pointing at a fat slice of carrot cake. "You're mine," she said. "Hey, Dee! You hear that? This carrot cake is mine. Don't go giving it to anyone else."

"Three pumps?" Dee asked, sliding Leah's drink across the counter in a wide white mug, settled on a large saucer with the muffin.

"You know it," Jasmine said. "And I've got my punch card, don't forget."

"I would never." The barista busied herself with Jasmine's order, finishing by tallying it up on the cash register. "With your punch card discount, that's seven eighty-five."

Jasmine slid a ten-dollar bill across the counter. "Keep the change." She wiggled her eyebrows at Leah, taking their tray. "Where shall we sit to discuss our dastardly deeds?"

"The window?"

"Perfect, we can people-watch."

"Is there much interesting behavior in a parking lot?" Leah asked, pulling out a chair for Jasmine.

"Oh, yeah, for sure," Jasmine said, setting the tray on the dark stained wooden table, small and square but perfect for two people. "People are feral when it comes to parking. Haven't you ever been to the Sparkling Lights festival in Roanoak Falls? I swear I almost saw a homicide about parking once."

"No, I've never been," Leah answered. "I've never had anyone to go with." The second part of the sentence dropped from her mouth before she could swallow it back, shoving it down where it belonged. "I mean, you know, it's busy at work this time of year."

Jasmine nodded, passing one of the mugs to Leah. "Record profits and a skeleton staff. Seems like it's the same every year."

"I thought you were new at Syndicorp." Leah blew across the mug, disturbing the neat tendrils of steam that lifted to the ceiling. "Did you transfer?"

"Nah, every place is the same," Jasmine said. "Doesn't matter where you are these days." She took a notepad from her messenger bag, placing a pink pen on top of a fresh, unmarked page. "Now, Leah, if we're going to pull this off, we'll need to know at least the basics about each other."

"Are you sure this is a good idea?" Leah asked, praying Jasmine would back out. "I mean, messing with your family, isn't that a bit... strange?"

"Trust me, this is for their own good." Jasmine tapped the notebook. "Write down something about yourself, and then I'll go. I thought writing might make it easier, plus then we'll have notes we can study from."

"What did you say you studied in college again?" Leah asked, sliding the notebook towards herself.

"I went to school to be an archivist," Jasmine supplied, stabbing her fork into a large chunk of the carrot cake. "But there's not much work for that around here."

Leah nodded, pink pen poised over the page but she couldn't think of a single thing to write.

"Just start anywhere," Jasmine said, poking her lightly in the arm. "Family, school, friends." She stuffed the carrot cake into her mouth, moaning quietly and rolling her eyes back in her head. "God, this is good." She chewed thoughtfully and swallowed. "Hobbies?"

"I go to the movies sometimes," Leah said, writing that down. "The worse they are, the more I enjoy myself."

"You like bad movies more than good ones?" Jasmine asked. "Why?"

"It takes a lot of courage to make something bad and put it out there anyway. While most of us are panicking that we're not good enough, some people are out there producing the worst garbage you can imagine and proudly putting their name on it." She tapped the pen against the paper, adding the name of her favorite bad film, *Kanga-phoon*. "I guess I wish I had that kind of bravery."

"Deep, Erickson," Jasmine said thoughtfully, nodding. "I like it." She took the notebook back, flipping to a blank page and writing several lines before setting the pen down. "I'm sorry that my first contribution isn't as personal or interesting, but it's probably for the best that you at least know everyone's name. They think we've been dating for three months, and I'd have been talking about them, you know."

Leah nearly choked on her hot chocolate, swallowing the wrong way and having to stop to cough into a napkin. "Three months?" she finally managed to eke out. "Me?"

"Well, not you specifically," Jasmine explained. "Just a mystery woman I've yet to divulge much about."

"So you've been lying for three months?"

"I told you, it's for their own good." Jasmine nudged the notebook towards Leah, giving her an encouraging grin. "They worry too much."

"About your love life?"

"About everything, when it comes to me." Jasmine's phone vibrated against the table, buzzing softly. She glanced at the notification and unlocked it, typing rapidly. "See? I'm gone for an hour and already my mother is asking when I ate last."

Leah looked down at the page, Jasmine's neat, loopy writing easily legible and pleasing to look at, even in the eye-searingly pink ink. "Mother is Anne— shouldn't I call her Mrs. Reed?"

"Not unless you want to hear a lecture," Jasmine said with a snort. "She'll insist you call her Annie." She pointed at each line of the page as she spoke. "You can probably go with Mr. Cross for my grandpa, at least at first. Obviously you know my name, but I wasn't sure if you knew my middle name."

"Lily?"

"My mom likes plants."

Leah nodded, staring down at the page. "What about this brother? The one you gave a kidney to?"

"He won't be there, and they won't mention him," Jasmine explained. "We shared a dad. Neither of them were around very much." She reached across the table, somehow managing to write upside-down on the paper. "But his name is Josh."

"I don't think my family is very notable," Leah said. "At least, not to me." She took another greedy gulp of the hot chocolate, savoring the sweet, minty taste that coated her tongue. "We don't talk much."

"Well, what else is there to know?" Jasmine prompted, pointing at the notebook again. "Come on, Leah, you have to give me something."

"Can't I just be the quiet, mysterious type?"

"If you go down that road, they're going to try prying you open with a crowbar." Jasmine scraped another forkful of cake from the plate, scraping the icing from the saucer. "They don't mean to pry, they're just... curious. And worried. And probably a little bit nosey, if we're being honest." Her phone buzzed again and she sighed, glancing at it. "And that's Mom again, asking why I'm all the way out here instead of in Rockland Heights." She slid the phone back into her pocket, silencing it. "Between you and me, the drinks here are much better."

"Not even a competition," Leah agreed.

"So how is that hot chocolate treating you?"

"Better than the dry packets I have at home," Leah admitted. "You know, the ones with the mini marshmallows?"

"You can't beat a good marshmallow, even if they are dehydrated." Jasmine licked the tines of her fork, leaving no trace of even one single crumb. "I wish I could eat that every day."

Leah nodded, staring out the window at a woman yelling at a man who'd parked too close to her. The woman's hat was wobbling angrily on her head, the pompom dangerously close to jumping ship into the muddy, melted ice water running from the snowdrift to the sewer grate. "Looks like you were right about the people watching," she said.

"If you could change anything about your life, what would it be?" Jasmine asked.

"Uh..."

"You know, if a genie or a wizard or something popped out of thin air and said, Leah Erickson, you get one wish, and one wish only, and it can't be money, what would it be?"

"Is this relevant?" Leah grumbled, nudging the notebook away from herself.

"It speaks to broader character."

"Why can't it be money? That would solve almost all of my problems immediately."

"Because," Jasmine said, now also watching the altercation in the parking lot. "It's a boring, obvious answer. Dig deeper!"

Leah swallowed hard, poking at the top of the muffin, sticky with its delicate clear glaze. "I wish Syndicorp would pay me more?"

"That's still wishing for more money, just with extra steps," Jasmine protested. "Come on, something heartfelt. Make it like a cheesy film on at Christmas." She stared over the rim of her mug, her sparkly white eyeliner glinting in the corners of her eyes. "Lie if you have to."

"Okay, uh…" Leah tried, failing to come up with an acceptable answer that would pass the arbitrary test. "I'd wish that I could experience all of my favorite things again for the first time."

Jasmine sat back in her chair, nodding. "That's a really good answer." She took the notebook, scrawling into the margins of the page.

"Wait, what are you doing?" Leah asked, reaching for it, but Jasmine easily kept it out of her reach.

"Taking notes, obviously."

"Why?"

"Because if we're going to pull this off, I need to have at least some idea of what makes you tick." She tucked the pen back into the safety of the spiral binding, clipping the edge so it wouldn't get lost. "You're deep water, Leah, I can just tell."

"Oh?"

Jasmine nodded. "Yup." Her eyes followed the two outside, still yelling about the parking space, despite there being several empty ones nearby. "So much for goodwill to all, and all that," she muttered. "Why can't people just be a little more relaxed this time of year?"

"My guess is all the extra stress," Leah offered. "No one has enough cash, everywhere is busy, some people plan forty-two-course meals and then freak out if something goes wrong."

"We only do forty-one courses, don't worry," Jasmine replied with a wink. "You haven't filled out much of the sheet yet," she protested. "I need more information about my mysterious, aloof girlfriend."

There was something in the way she said it that sent butterflies alight in Leah's stomach, but she cleared her throat, deciding to ignore it. They were embarking on a business transaction, nothing more. She'd get the time off she needed, and Jasmine would get a little space from her family. It was perfect, really, aside from the family part. That much twisted her gut into a knot. "I don't know, maybe this isn't a good idea."

"What isn't a good idea? Watching World War Three unfold in the parking lot?" Jasmine asked, laughing.

Leah shook her head. "No, I mean the deal," she said. "It doesn't feel right to be deceiving your family this way."

"Doesn't your family ever ask too many questions?" Jasmine swallowed the rest of her hot chocolate, glancing around for the barista, or maybe for a garbage can. "Don't you ever wish you could escape, but know you'd miss them even a couple of minutes later?"

"No," Leah answered truthfully. "It's hard to miss people who were never really there in the first place."

Jasmine nodded, returning to her mug. "I get that." Then, she tapped the notebook insistently, putting on a mocking stern expression. "Come on, Erickson. We have work to do."

Chapter Four

Jasmine tossed her bag onto the kitchen island, heaving herself atop the stool with a thud, the hardwood squeaking beneath the legs. "Hey, I'm home," she announced, stating the obvious.

"Hey's for horses," her mother said, scrubbing at the grout between the tiles. "How was the cafe?"

"Fine," Jasmine replied, not really willing to give her any more information than that. "Good."

"That's it?"

"Yep, that's it."

Searching, her mother stared at her, but finding nothing, returned to the brush in her hands. "Did you eat?"

"Yes, I ate. It was an enormous slice of carrot cake. There were even walnuts in it, and because they love me there, no raisins." Jasmine took the brush, taking a turn at scrubbing, the bristles already bent and mostly useless. "How was your day?"

"You only had cake? Nothing else?" Her mother turned towards the refrigerator, hunting through the crisper drawer. "Jazzy, you know you need to eat a balanced diet, and I'm not sure that cake is at the top of the list."

"I'm fine, Mom, I had eggs and stuff this morning." Jasmine waved her away, along with the head of lettuce she was holding out. "What do you expect me to do, chow down on some iceberg? I'm not a rabbit."

"Iceberg isn't actually very nutritionally complete for rabbits," her mother retorted, still holding it out.

"If it doesn't make a difference for rabbits, what makes you think it's going to help me?" Jasmine shot back, grinning, because she knew she'd won the argument.

Her mother glared at her. "Fine," she said, returning the lettuce to the fridge. "But I hope you're sticking around for dinner. Grandpa is making that thing he likes."

"What thing?"

"You know, that hearty stew he always raves about." Her mother nodded towards the slow cooker on the counter. "Should be ready soon, if you're hungry after your cake."

"Always hungry for stew," Jasmine said, knowing she wouldn't win that battle twice in a row. "Where is he, anyway?"

"Oh, you know," her mother said, waving her hand in the air. "Out in the garage with his rocks. Says the new batch is a good one. Between you and me, I'm tired of these shiny things collecting dust all over the house." She plucked a small tigerseye from the windowsill, where it was glinting gently in the afternoon light. "Tons of these things. Everywhere. And this was the man who always chastised me for collecting shells at the beach." Her mother shook her head, bemused. "I suppose we should be grateful he has a hobby other than sleeping in that damned chair in the living room."

"It's a good chair," Jasmine defended. "Haven't you ever dozed off in it?"

"No, your grandfather is always in residence when I'm in there." Her mother chortled quietly, taking back the scrub brush. "Have you given any more thought to bringing this girlfriend around for Christmas?" she asked. "I know she probably has her own plans, you said as much, but—"

"Yep, she's coming," Jasmine said casually, avoiding eye contact and choosing instead to inspect the peeling edges of the vinyl sun catcher on the windowpane that was casting little beams of rainbow across the white tiles.

"She is?" her mother asked excitedly. "She is!" Bustling around the kitchen, she started to point at various tasks that needed to be done. "We'll need to scrub down the cabinets, that laminate is starting to look dingy. Oh, and I'll ask Grandpa to finish redoing the trim on the landing, and—oh, Jazzy, does she have any allergies? Is there anything she doesn't like?"

"Uh…" Jasmine stumbled, her heart beginning to thud dully in her chest. They hadn't discussed any of that. It wasn't in her notes. "No?"

"You're not sure?"

"Well she's never gone into anaphylactic shock in my presence, so I'm guessing not." Jasmine tapped out a frantic text to Leah, starting it with *S.O.S.* so it wouldn't be ignored. "I'll ask her."

"I don't want anyone visiting the emergency room on Christmas," her mother scolded. "I want everyone to have a nice day. What does she like? Maybe we should get her a gift, or—"

"No, Mom," Jasmine interrupted. "No gifts. Just be chill."

"Be chill," her mother repeated, brow furrowed. "I don't know if I can manage to *be chill* on one of my favorite days of the year."

"Try," Jasmine said, just as her phone pinged with Leah's reply. "She's not allergic to anything."

"Does she like carrots? You know, those glazed carrots I like to make, should I make those? Or if not, maybe a green bean casserole? That's assuming she has no aversions to mushrooms, though, and I'm aware that—"

"Mom!" Jasmine almost shouted, regretting it almost instantly. "Just relax, okay? I told her you wouldn't be too wild. I promised her it would be low-key."

Her mother wrinkled her nose, tossing the brush into a sink full of cold suds. "I'm not sure if I've ever been low-key even once in my life."

"No, Annie, you haven't," her grandfather said, patting her mother on the shoulder as he entered from the garage. "But you keep this place ticking, so we'll let it slide."

Jasmine scooted off the stool, accepting his embrace. "Hey Paps. How are the rocks?"

"Oh you know, rocky," he replied, pausing to laugh at his own joke. "Heh. Rocky." He lifted the lid of the slow cooker, inhaling deeply. "What's this I eavesdropped about a girlfriend coming for Christmas?"

"Only if you two promise to not make it weird," Jasmine said, pointing a finger at him playfully. "I mean it, don't scare her off by being too intense, or asking too many questions. She's shy." That much, at least, was the truth. Leah barely said ten words unless provoked or cajoled into it.

"Alright, alright," he relented, setting the lid back down. "I won't ask her when she's proposing, is that the idea?"

"Paps, I will throw you out into the snow myself," Jasmine teased, making sure he knew she was a little bit serious. "If either of you make it weird, I promise I will never bring anyone home for the holidays ever again." She picked up the wooden spoon that he'd abandoned on the counter, gesturing at both of them. "I mean it."

Her mother took the wooden spoon, setting it on top of a plate so that the broth wouldn't splash over the freshly cleaned counters. "Okay, Jazzy, we hear you," she said. "We just worry about you, you know, with your health conditions—"

"That was ten years ago, Mom," Jasmine protested. "Clean bill of health. Fit as a fiddle or whatever."

"It's not as though you've been seeing anyone since that Danielle," her mother continued. "It's been a while, and we just want to see you happy."

Jasmine groaned, burying her face in her hands. "Why did you have to bring up Danielle?" she asked, her voice muffled. "She moved away two years ago."

"And broke your heart," her mother added, making a small tut in the back of her throat. "We never even got to meet her."

"And look at that, it didn't matter," Jasmine said, taking three large bowls from the cabinet, each of them with a different pattern. A chip in the ceramic rubbed roughly against her skin as she set them out next to the pot. "You two worry too much."

Her mother leaned over the slow cooker, sinking a ladle that looked like the Loch Ness monster beneath the tomatoey surface. "I shouldn't have to explain why that is," she said, drawing it back up filled with tender potatoes, beef, and carrots. "You were sick for so long."

"And now I'm not," Jasmine said, shrugging her off and taking the bowl. The heat radiated through the patterning, absorbing into her hands. "And Danielle was..." she paused to sit at the kitchen table, digging into the stew with a large spoon. "A mistake."

"I know it's hard to date here," her mother said. "Trust me, I know. Not one eligible bachelor for fifty miles, according to that app you put on my phone."

"Apps, computers, nonsense," her grandfather scoffed, filling his own bowl, making sure to take extra carrots, his favorite. "It's no wonder love is dead in the modern age. I met your grandmother—"

"At Woodstock, Paps, I know, you've told me at least a million times." She savored the hearty taste, letting it fill her mouth and delight her taste buds for a moment before she swallowed. "We can't all meet the loves of our lives at a concert."

Her grandfather walked his dish to the table, sloshing over the sides because he'd overfilled it. He sopped up the drips with the toe of his sock, ignoring the tuts from the women present. "How many concerts have you been to, Jazzy?" he asked. "Can't know if you never try."

"Paps, have you seen the cost of tickets these days?" she asked, laughing. "They're practically the cost of your first mortgage payment." She sliced a potato in half with the edge of her spoon and positioned it with several crushed tomatoes before devouring the bite. "Besides, it's not like the best bands are coming to Rockland Heights, of all places. We're lucky to get a mediocre cover band at the local bar every now and then."

He sat down, the chair legs scraping noisily against the floor. "I drove for sixteen hours to get to Woodstock," he said again for the thousandth time. "It was the best decision I ever made."

"Great, find me a historical concert that changes the face of the music industry within a sixteen-hour drive, and I'll gas up the old car and go." Jasmine dragged her spoon through the remaining thick broth at the bottom of her bowl, scooping and then slurping it up. "Good stew, Paps," she said, standing to wash her bowl in the sink. "As usual." She took her mother's dish, washing that one, too, her shoulder blades stiffening at the thought of what would come next in the conversation. "So the new job," she started, being sure to keep her eyes fixed on the rapidly encroaching darkness outside, avoiding even looking at the reflections in the glass. "I've been fine working the longer shifts."

"That's good," her mother said cautiously, standing to pass her the final dish. "Maybe in a few months, when you're more used to it, you can think about asking for more hours."

"It's a skeleton crew, Mom, there won't be more hours."

Her mother shrugged, dropping the bowl into the suds. "It might pick up."

"I applied to a job at the big reserve downstate," Jasmine said quickly, and the icy film of apprehension filled the room as soon as the words slipped past her lips. "It's a good fit for me, and—"

"I don't think that's a good idea, Jazzy," her mother said, taking the sponge from her. "What if something happened? What if—"

"Nothing is going to happen!" Jasmine protested, finding her hands on her hips in a petulant stance that was almost certainly undermining her point. "I haven't had any complications for three or four years, Mom. I'm fine. Out of the woods, or whatever."

"You and I both know issues can crop up at any time. Dr. Ahara said that you need to be careful now, and stressing yourself with such a big move isn't what she meant." Her mother reached out to lay a hand on Jasmine's shoulder, but she shook it off.

"I don't want to spend the next ten years working for Syndicorp," Jasmine replied. "I can't build a foundation for my life on the shifting sands of their scheduling." She backed up to the wall, feeling cornered, leaning against the peeling wallpaper and the pencil marks on the door frame, marking her height as she'd grown up. "I went to school to be an archivist, and I want to at least try to make that happen."

"How far downstate?" her grandfather asked from the table, his hands folded atop the crocheted placemat. "What are the medical facilities like down there?"

"A few hours," Jasmine said. "That's all. And yes, thank you, they do have a regional hospital, and—"

"It's too far from the city," her mother said firmly, doing her best to shut down the conversation. "If, heaven forbid, something did happen, you'd never get transferred to a better department in time. All of your specialists are up here, your entire team."

"None of whom I've seen in years, because I've been fine," Jasmine challenged. "I know that you're worried, Mom, but—"

"It goes far past worry, Jasmine. Nearly a decade of fretting in hospital corridors, eating lunch out of vending machines, always worried about one more surgery, one more complication, all the time terrified it would take you away from me forever, all because you gave that lousy brother of yours a kidney."

Jasmine ducked away from another attempt at a hug, now standing in the doorway. "It was mine to give," she shot back. "And even now, even after all of this, I don't regret it, not for a minute, because I would rather that Damien be alive and annoying out on the West Coast than still be on a waiting list, or worse, dead."

"He didn't deserve your sacrifice!" her mother barked, tears filling her eyes. "You haven't even seen him in years, Jazzy, and he never even sent a card for any of your operations. Not a single bouquet of flowers, not—"

"You think I care about flowers?" Jasmine barked. "I don't care about any of that. He's my brother, and he needed me."

"Half-brother," her mother corrected. "And I don't recall your father even bothering to get tested to see if he was a match."

"All the more reason that it was right for me to offer," Jasmine said softly. "It's not Damien's fault that I had so many problems after, and it's not his fault that he didn't, and it's not his fault that Dad took off on him, too."

"He should have been more grateful," her mother said, the firmness of her tone ricocheting off the tiles. "He should have stayed here."

"What's the sense in ruining two lives?" Jasmine asked. "What's the point of that? He wants to be a pro-surfer, he needs to be out there for that. It's not like he can be a surfer when the only water within hundreds of miles are lakes. What was he supposed to do, try to ride the wake of a pontoon boat?"

"He was supposed to stay here and at least care that your sacrifice ruined your life," her mother said. "He should have apologized, and he should have stayed." She threw her hands up, tossing the sponge into the drying rack. "It never should have been your life that was ruined." She turned on her heel, marching out into the garage and slamming the door behind her.

"Great," Jasmine said under her breath. "Just great."

"She needs some time, Jazzy," her grandfather said, unfurling a newspaper noisily. "She spent a long time doing nothing other than worrying about you, and she doesn't know how to turn it off."

"That's not my fault," Jasmine retorted. "I should be allowed to make my own decisions without her flying off the handle about Damien."

"It's complicated, Flower." He shrugged helplessly, laying the paper down on the table to yank out the comic section. "What's the job?"

"Archivist for elements found at the park," she said, heaving out a sigh. "I just know she'll never speak to me again if I go."

Her grandfather folded the comics, pocketing them for later. "I'll work on her," he said. "In the meantime, you start preparing for that interview you're going to get, alright?"

"Yeah," Jasmine said. "Alright."

Chapter Five

Leah raised her hand to knock on the door, wondering if it was too late to back out. Her car was still parked down the street, if she ran, no one would know she'd even been there in the first place. She took a step backward off the porch, preparing to sprint through the slush to freedom. She'd get fired for missing those shifts without cover, but she could find another job... probably.

Despite her knuckles still poised in the air, the door opened, revealing an older man with a white ponytail, his overalls covered in something that looked like sawdust.

"Can I help you?" he asked, polite and friendly.

"Uh, no, actually—" Leah began, until he spied her duffel bag.

"Oh!" he shouted, leaning out onto the porch. "Are you the girlfriend? You must be her—Annie!" he yelled into the next room, cupping his hands around his mouth. "Annie, she's here!"

"Who's here?" Annie—Jasmine's mother—replied from the other room, sounding distracted. "Dad, you said you'd help me with some of this food preparation, what are you doing out there?"

He stuck his hand out, knuckles calloused from years of hard work. "I'm Jasmine's grandfather. You can call me Martin."

"Leah," she replied, shaking his hand. Her heart was already pounding in her chest, an inescapable symptom of the crushing anxiety that was pooling readily in her lungs.

"Pleased to make your acquaintance," he said, stepping out of the way and gesturing for her to enter. "Annie, it's Jasmine's girlfriend," he said, locking the front door. "Jasmine!" he yelled up the stairs. "Leah is here!" He picked up Leah's duffel, taking it up the uncarpeted stairs. "Boots on the shelf there if you please, Leah," he said. "It gets pretty messy otherwise."

Leah slipped off her boots, part of her wishing she could carry them under her arm, a reminder that she could leave whenever she wanted, but that wouldn't help her look like a normal, stable girlfriend. She wasn't one of those, of course, but she should at least try. "Of course," she said, sliding her boots onto the shelf, muddy water already dripping into the grooved plastic tray below.

"We didn't think you'd be here for another day or two," he said from the top of the stairs, leaning against the banister. "I for one am thrilled we get a little more time to get to know you."

"Oh, uh, me too," Leah replied, cursing herself internally for not pushing back on Jasmine's insistence they arrive on the twenty-second of December, instead of the twenty-fourth. But neither of them had any shifts, and Jasmine was very persuasive with those enormous brown eyes of hers, pleading, sparkling when she got her way.

"You're here!" Jasmine shrieked, throwing open her bedroom door. She paused, like she didn't know what to do next, before she wrapped Leah in a tight embrace, kissing her on the cheek. "You must have made good time, I thought the traffic would have been a nightmare this time of day."

"I got lucky, I guess," Leah replied, wishing she was still staring at a stranger's tail lights. "I didn't want to be late."

"Are you hungry?" Jasmine asked, setting the blue canvas duffel on the floor near the closet, the sliding doors mirrored and closed.

Leah nodded. Her hunger always ramped up the closer she got to a full moon, leaving her ravenous most months. Cheap packs of noodles rarely filled the insatiable void within her for longer than a few minutes at most. "Yeah, I could eat," she said. "I'm sorry, I didn't bring anything. I should have, that was rude."

Martin clapped a hand on her shoulder, beaming brightly. "Don't be silly! You're our guest until Christmas!" he chastised gently. "Although I will admit, Annie might not say no to help with the baking tomorrow. My daughter is a gingerbread machine. Do you like gingerbread, Leah?"

"Er—"

Jasmine wrapped her arms around Leah's waist from behind, resting her chin on Leah's shoulder. "I thought we could go to the Sparkling Lights festival in Roanoak Falls tonight," she said, fingers interlaced over Leah's stomach. "What do you think, babe?"

"Festival?" Leah squeaked, her abs tensing under Jasmine's light touch. Her thoughts raced between something like a blaring alarm and the inextricable desire to jump out the second-floor window, hit the ground running, and never look back.

"Yeah, the one I told you about, silly! They have the best corndogs you'll ever taste, I swear. And flavored popcorn, too, if you like that. Paps here is a total fiend for their boozy hot chocolate. Don't worry, Mom is the designated driver! Safety first, and all that." She exhaled a light laugh through her nose, and her breath ghosted across Leah's ear.

"Do you have a bathroom?" Leah asked, wriggling from Jasmine's grip. "I mean, of course you have a bathroom, I'm just wondering if it's okay for you to tell me where it is?" She smacked herself on the forehead, aware that she was already messing everything up. "Sorry, I drank a lot of water after my shift this morning."

Martin tilted his head, bemused. "Last door on the left," he said, gesturing down the short hallway. "First door on the left is the linen closet for towels and things."

"Thanks," Leah said, escaping into the sanctuary of the dated bathroom, the avocado green fixtures strangely quaint when they should have looked dull and worn out. Tiled floor-to-ceiling in crisp white squares, several plants draped their hanging leaves over the side of the windowsill, dangling down next to the pedestal sink. She sat on the edge of the tub, moving the shower curtain to one side.

"Breathe, Leah," she whispered to herself, burying her face in her hands. "Breathe. It's only a few days. At least her family already knows that she's gay, it's not like this is some grand coming out scheme."

There was a soft knock on the pine door. "Are you okay?" Jasmine whispered. "Paps went back to the garage to finish something before we leave."

"Yeah, all fine," Leah lied, scowling at her reddened reflection. She opened the door as she ran a hand through her hair, pushing it to one side for the tenth time since she'd entered the house. "What's up?"

Jasmine closed the door again, standing across the bathroom a distance away, folding and unfolding her arms. "Sorry, I meant to be the one to answer the door."

Leah shrugged, her leather jacket still on, the zippers quietly rattling. "It's fine."

"They're just excited to meet you," Jasmine offered, taking a cautious step forward. "We don't have to go to the festive fair if you'd rather not."

"You said they have corndogs?" Leah asked, trying for a smile. It was just a few days, and then it would be all over. She'd never have to see this girl's family ever again. "I could go for a corndog."

Jasmine beamed, biting her lip in excitement. "Great! I think we'll head out soon, it's about an hour's drive from here. Paps will drive out and Mom will drive us back, so if you want to have one of those hot chocolates, you should." Her brow furrowed. "I probably should have asked if you drink, first."

"Occasionally," Leah replied. She inhaled slowly, willing her muscles to release their death grip around her tendons. "This hot chocolate sounds good." She adjusted the shower curtain, sliding the plastic rings across the vintage metal rail that was bolted into the wall, the brackets rusted at the edges.

"I'll give you the tour," Jasmine offered, opening the door again. "This is the main bathroom, obviously," she said, stepping out onto the carpet runner that spanned the width of the hallway. "And this is my room." She stole a glance back at Leah, her face scrunched up. "Did you want to unpack?"

"Uh—"

"Come on, I'll help you," Jasmine said, ushering Leah inside and latching the door. "I hope it's okay that you stay in here. I should have mentioned it, but I assumed Mom would expect you to sleep on the pull-out sofa in the den. It wasn't until an hour or so ago that she insisted we stay in the same room." Jasmine threw out her arms helplessly as she sat on the edge of her bed. "She's adamant that she's okay with the whole lesbian thing, so adamant that she's practically been begging me to get a girlfriend for years."

Leah chewed on her tongue, trying and failing to find the right words to say. "I snore sometimes," she said finally.

"That's okay, so do I." Jasmine nodded at the duffel bag on the thin green carpet, worn from years of someone standing in front of the closet doors. "You can hang stuff up if you want."

"I only brought jeans and stuff," Leah mumbled. "A few shirts. A sweater."

"The shirts?" Jasmine suggested, sliding open the closet to reveal a moderately organized collection of clothes, with dresses on the far left, including a long white one with lace sleeves. Jasmine frowned at it, shoving it to the edge of the rail, hiding it with the adjacent garments. "I have a few hangers spare."

Leah nodded, unzipping her bag and taking out the three plaid shirts she had packed: one red, and two green. "Thanks," she said, hanging them next to Jasmine's. Something about the way they were nestled together in there sparked something in her gut that she vowed to ignore.

"Very festive, Erickson," Jasmine approved, adjusting a few notebooks on her small, cramped desk. "I'll sleep on the floor, okay?"

"No," Leah argued, shaking her head. "It's your house. I'll sleep on the floor."

"But you're my guest," Jasmine challenged, her hands now on her hips. "Don't argue with me, you won't win. Haven't you heard about Midwestern hospitality?"

"Aren't there usually salads with marshmallows in?" Leah teased.

Jasmine snorted a laugh. "God, don't let my mom hear you say that, the woman is obsessed with ambrosia salad. I hate to be the bearer of bad news, but there will definitely be marshmallows on the sweet potatoes."

"I love marshmallows, so that's hardly a threat." Leah slid the door closed and leaned against it, tugging at the edges of her jacket. "And I'm sleeping on the floor. I'm the one who asked for a favor in the first place, I initiated this whole thing, so there are no more arguments, Reed." She closed up her bag, keeping her stash of granola bars hidden from prying eyes. No doubt Jasmine wouldn't understand why she was so ravenous, even after eating a normal quantity of food for a human her size.

"We'll revisit this tomorrow," Jasmine warned with a mischievous glint in her eye. "But fine, yes, for tonight I'll let you sleep on the floor."

"You'll *let* me?" Leah asked, laughing. She was grateful for her natural warmth as the temperature plummeted, icing over the concrete where it met the frozen grass. "I don't think we will be revisiting this, actually."

Jasmine arched an eyebrow, perched at the edge of her bed and fluffing one of the decorative pillows, knitted and shaped like a giant rainbow. "I have my ways."

"Nice cushion." Leah gestured at the rainbow, bemused. "I didn't expect your interior design skills to be so heavy on the... on that."

"Mom made it. She took up knitting a few years ago and loves any excuse. I like a more minimalist vibe, but that's not going to happen in this house." Jasmine tossed it at Leah and leaned back on the bed, stretching her arms over her head. "It's been good for her, I think. Everyone needs a hobby, and at least this one helps with her anxiety."

"Maybe I should take it up, too," Leah replied, alarmed at the words that had just come out of her mouth. "I, uh—I just mean because who doesn't need enormous rainbow pillows, right?"

"I think everyone needs at least two," Jasmine agreed, graciously ignoring the rest of the statement. "Three, if you're lucky. I bet my Mom would make you one if you asked."

"I don't know if three days is going to cut it, do you?" Leah brushed her fingertips over the ridged texture, each little bump a stitch. The colors were vibrant and solid, and only a little scratchy.

"Oh," Jasmine said, sitting back up. "Yeah, I mean, no, of course, three days probably isn't enough. I think this one took her at least a week, if I'm right about all her furtive crafting around my birthday last summer."

"Furtive crafting," Leah replied, tossing the pillow back. "I suppose there are worse things in life, right?"

"Jazzy, we're about ready to go," Annie shouted from downstairs. "Is Leah coming with?"

"Yeah," Jasmine yelled back, opening the door. "She was just unpacking. We'll be right down."

"Tell her to bundle up, it's supposed to get cold tonight!"

Jasmine glanced over at Leah in her leather jacket and frowned. "Is that all you have?"

"I'll be fine," Leah reassured her. "I run hot."

"Hot enough to not freeze at night in a leather jacket and what, a plaid shirt?" Jasmine unlatched the lid of an oak trunk at the foot of her bed, digging down past thick wool blankets and extra pillows, resurfacing with a tacky festive sweater and what looked like a hand-knitted wool hat with a comically large pompom hanging from the crown. "Here," she said, tossing both items at Leah. "I believe you, but my mother won't, and I'm guessing you don't want her hovering over us all evening."

Leah dropped her jacket on the ground, pulling the sweater on. "I don't think I've looked this ready for the holidays since I was about eight years old," she said, suppressing the scowl ready to plaster itself across her face. The sweater featured a large reindeer head, the stitches uneven and lumpy, the length short enough that the blue plaid of her button-down peeked out at the bottom. The large, red nose was made of shiny shreds of thread, and it was already shedding all over the navy blue background. "I love it," she announced, tugging the hat over her ears. "Did your mom make this, too?"

"One of her first creations. She's gotten much better since she joined that group at the library." Jasmine grabbed Leah's hand, tugging her out of the bedroom and down the stairs so quickly, that Leah barely had time to rescue her jacket from the floor, zipping it up over the bulky sweater.

"You must be Leah," Jasmine's mother said, jingling the car keys in her hand, and twirling the ring around her index finger. "I'd love to say that we've heard so much about you, but I'm afraid that's not true." She smiled but shot a look at Jasmine, who deftly ignored it.

"Don't harass her, Annie," Martin said, buttoning his thick peacoat. "She's only been here for five minutes and you're trying to give her the third degree."

Annie held her hands up in surrender, motioning for the rest of them to exit through the open door. "We'd better get going," she said. "I don't want to drive all the way out to Roanoak Falls just to find out that they've sold out of corndogs for the night."

Chapter Six

Jasmine made a point to sit as close to Leah as she could in the back seat, holding onto her arm like it was the last lifeboat in the ocean. If they were going to get away with their innocent little scam, it had to look believable. She grinned at her grandfather in the rear-view mirror, leaning her head onto Leah's shoulder.

Her grandfather parked the car alongside several others, staring up at the street lamp above. "Alright, people, don't forget, we're parked under this sign that says no parking." He turned off the engine and handed the keys to Jasmine's mother, who was staring at him with a concerned expression. "Don't look at me like that," he said, waving her off. "It's only during school hours."

"You'd better hope you're right, old man," her mother retorted, climbing out of the passenger seat. "I don't want another ticket."

"We're not going to get a ticket!" he protested, tugging a matching hat down over his ears. "What shall we say, two hours? Three?"

Jasmine's mother checked her wristwatch, and then her phone. "Three," she confirmed. "I want to take my time looking at the ice sculptures."

"Ice sculptures?" Leah asked, breaking her silence.

Jasmine poked her gently in the side as she stepped out of the back seat. "Of course, silly. I'll show you. Food first or art first?" she asked.

"Art," her mother said, marching off towards the fair, purpose-driven to see what she'd come to see.

"I'm meeting an old friend for that hot chocolate," her grandfather said, pulling his coat tight around himself. "Are you two going to be okay on your own?"

"I think we'll manage, Paps," Jasmine said with a theatrical roll of her eyes. "Go on, enjoy your fancy drink. I think I should get Leah some food first."

Leah's stomach growled in reply, and she coughed awkwardly in a desperate attempt to hide it.

"I heard that," Jasmine said, holding out a mittened hand. She leaned in, whispering in Leah's ear. "Come on, we should look cute. It's more convincing that way."

"Alright," Leah said, following suit. "How far to these famed corn dogs, then?"

Jasmine pointed up a lit path, twinkling lights sparkling against untouched snow, cordoned off by thick velvet-like ropes. "Not far," she answered. "Did you eat at all today?"

"No," Leah said. "Too nervous I'd mess everything up."

"So far, you're doing great. Very believable, ten out of ten acting skills." Jasmine tugged her closer, seeing her grandfather peer at them from his place at the back of the line for hot chocolate. "But giving a more thorough performance can't hurt."

"How about an appetizer?" Leah suggested, pointing at the popcorn stand with her free hand. "You said they have flavors?"

"Oh yeah, all kinds," Jasmine said excitedly. "If you're really brave, you can ask them to mix a bunch of them together for an extremely wild experience. One bite sweet, the next spicy, the next savory, or salty, or—" she cut herself off with a laugh, covering her mouth and marring the cloud of vapor that lingered at her lips. "Sorry. I'm just really glad you're here." The words came so easily, and felt so honest, yet she regretted them almost instantly. They were acting, nothing more. She kicked a clump of snow off the path, where it exploded into a fine dust that glittered in the night air. "I just mean I think this might help them realize that I'm okay now. I'm fine, healthy, they don't have to worry all the time."

"And if this works, what will you do with all your newfound freedom?" Leah asked, playing with the zipper of her jacket. "Take over the world? Cure diseases? Discover something new?”

“I don’t think I have the work ethic to take over the world,” Jasmine said. “And my organic chemistry test scores were nothing to write home about, if I’m honest.” She positioned them at the back of the line for popcorn, behind several other couples angling towards the mistletoe off to the left. Jasmine skirted them to the right. “I don’t know, is there anything left to be discovered?”

“Deep sea?” Leah offered, squinting at the menu. “Lots of terrifying stuff down there.”

“I’ll pass, thank you,” Jasmine said. “Too scary for me. I don’t even like B horror films.”

Leah turned towards her, face lit up like a tree. “What?” she gasped. “No. No, this cannot stand, I’m going to get you to watch one with me. I promise I’ll pick one that’s not as scary.”

“Are we brokering another deal?” Jasmine asked. “Do I get to ask for another favor?”

“What, pretending to be your girlfriend for three days isn’t enough?” Leah leaned forward onto the balls of her feet, mouthing the words on the menu. “Does that say sriracha?”

“It does.”

“Damn,” she said. “That sounds incredible.” She stepped forward in line, still gazing at the board behind the stand. “What kind of favor?”

Jasmine laughed, but it came out nervous, much to her own surprise. “I, uh... hadn’t really thought about it. How about an I-owe-you?”

“I’m not in the habit of writing blank checks,” Leah replied. “I could cover some shifts for you?”

“I’m already trying to hang onto the ones I’ve got.” Jasmine dug in her pocket for her wallet, fumbling with the snap through her mittens.

“I’ve got it,” Leah said, not even looking over at her. “Don’t worry.”

“I’m not worried, I’m just trying to be a good host. You already insisted on being the one to sleep on the floor,” Jasmine argued. “Let me get the popcorn, Erickson.”

Leah nodded, but there was a glint in her eye, a hint of something either mysterious, mischievous, or dangerous. "This is a dynamic that could extend in perpetuity, you know."

"Okay, new deal. I'll watch a terrible movie with you, but then I'm subjecting you to movie musicals." Jasmine squeezed Leah's hand. "Deal?"

Leah groaned, throwing her head back in anguish. "I hate musicals. Fine. Deal."

"We'll get the mix," Jasmine ordered. "Heavy on the sriracha." The attendant nodded, starting to fill a large, striped paper bag with small shovels of popcorn from each bin. Toffee, peanut butter, cheddar, mango and lime, topped with a heap of sriracha, the red kernels looking especially festive. He handed over the bag, taking Jasmine's cash and returning several coins in change.

Leah guided them to a bench near the start of the ice sculpture trail and began to dig into the snack. "I love this," she said. "This is the best thing I've eaten all week."

"And we're not even to the best part yet," Jasmine offered, removing her mittens and taking a handful from the bag. "I'm glad you wanted to come."

"I have to fulfill my duties, don't I?" Leah asked, crunching on more popcorn. "It wouldn't be a very fair deal if I welched on coming to this festival." She ate another handful one kernel at a time before she spoke again. "Do you come here every year?"

Jasmine nodded. "Just about. We missed a few years about a decade back, though."

"Why's that?"

"I was sick." Jasmine picked a piece of the toffee out, her favorite, and paired it with a cheddar. "Even when I wasn't in the hospital, my mom thought it was too dangerous for me to be out in the cold. I don't know, maybe she was right."

"You think so?" Leah probed. Tufts of blond hair poked out from under the hat, spiky in the cold but framing her face regardless.

"I don't know. Probably." Jasmine stole a piece from Leah's hand, tossing her an unapologetic grin. "Wild horses couldn't keep me away from this place now."

"Yeah, I see why. This popcorn is going to change my life." Leah laughed, funneling more into her mouth. "You were right to get the mix."

"I've never seen anyone eat it quite like that," Jasmine replied with a soft snort. "Most people hate the full mix of all the flavors."

Leah tilted her head back, looking up at the unobstructed stars above, far from any city's light pollution, marred only by the light of the waxing moon. "I'm not most people," she said.

"I can tell," Jasmine replied, her voice just a little too earnest, so she had to dirty it with a joke. "You haven't even barfed yet."

"Nope, I'm invincible," Leah said proudly. "I could eat just about anything and not get sick. I'm like a human garbage disposal." She offered the remaining popcorn to Jasmine, who declined, and then shook the bag into her mouth until every last kernel was gone. "That was amazing. What's next?"

"The sculptures, I guess?" Jasmine suggested, standing up off the bench. She dusted off the back pockets of her jeans, having accumulated powdery bits of snow and ice left on the wrought iron. Lights were strung over the path, twinkling in the darkness with their warm, inviting glow. It was only the first night, and true, they hadn't spent much time around her family yet, but they'd settled into each other's company far easier than she'd thought.

"You know," Jasmine said, linking arms with Leah and inching closer to absorb her warmth, "I didn't think you'd say yes to my little proposal. I was even more surprised when you showed up at the cafe two days ago."

Leah nodded, staring up at the lights, allowing Jasmine to creep in closer. "I told you, I was in a tight spot. I needed those shifts covered."

"Still, most people would have told me to take a hike with an ask like that." Jasmine tugged her gently along the paved path, neatly shoveled and salted, the displaced snow stacked into tiny drifts at the edges of the concrete, reflecting the blue glow from the sculptures. "Offered something else, or hell, just quit Syndicorp entirely."

"Would if I could," Leah replied, stopping to take in the sights of an enormous sculpture of a grizzly bear, life-sized and impressive. "I wonder how much ice sculpturists make? Maybe that can be my next career."

"What, shoving cans onto a shelf while Mrs. Campbell yells at you over your earpiece isn't soothing your soul or giving you a grand purpose in life?" Jasmine asked sarcastically. "It's a nice sculpture, though. This artist does a bear every year, must be a passion project or something. Sadly, I don't think that the town pays the artists. I don't imagine they could if they wanted to."

"Yeah, but imagine how cool it must feel to carve a huge block of ice with a chainsaw," Leah said, miming the motion and laughing. "I'd probably wind up in the emergency room."

"I think if my mother saw me with a chainsaw, she'd have a heart attack and we'd still wind up in the emergency room." Jasmine snapped a photo of the bear with her phone, frowning at the poor quality. "This phone sucks in low light," she grumbled.

"Try adjusting your settings," said a woman behind her. "And stay as still as possible, the shutter will stay open longer to compensate." She holstered her large camera, offering her hand. "Andie."

"Thanks, Andie," Jasmine said. "Leah, stay still. I'm going to use you as a tripod." She lined up the shot, balancing her phone on Leah's shoulder, standing on her toes to see the frame. She took the picture, this one much clearer than the last. "Cool. Thanks!"

The woman nodded, wandering off towards a group calling to her, yelling excitedly about the hot chocolate stand.

"You know, that boozy hot chocolate is starting to sound good," Leah said, bumping her shoulder against Jasmine's. "Maybe it's time to see if your grandpa is serious about all this." She pulled out her wallet, black leather and utilitarian, already selecting a ten-dollar bill from inside. "I'm paying this time, Reed, you can't stop me."

Jasmine held up her hands in surrender, the inch of skin between her parka and her mittens already uncomfortably cold. "I wouldn't dare," she said before nodding to a path on the side. "The stand was down on the other side last year. It's probably there again."

"I can't believe I've never been here before," Leah said as they joined the line for the hot chocolate. The brightly colored sign reading *Moonsugar* swung overhead in the evening's light breeze, and a selection of cupcakes graced the display case. "I guess I never had anyone to go with."

"No girlfriends?" Jasmine asked, aware that she was maybe too keenly interested in the answer. "No cute outings at Christmas?"

"If I had a girlfriend, do you think she would have been fine with me pretending to be yours for the holidays?" Leah asked, chortling under her breath. "No girlfriend. Not this year, and not last year, either. Not around the holidays, anyway."

"Summer fling?" Jasmine prodded, her eyes already fixed on a particularly glorious cake behind the glass, festooned with a tiny candy cane.

Leah gave her a sideways glance that was more of a grimace. "Yeah, I guess you could say that. She was heading off to some yoga retreat out west. It was a fun couple of weeks, I guess." She shuffled her boots against the salty sidewalk, the sound coarse but familiar. "I don't think we would have worked out, long-term."

"Why's that?" Jasmine asked.

"Amber enjoys the public eye too much for me, I think." Leah stepped forward as the line moved, still clutching the money in her hands. How she wasn't half-frozen with her coat unzipped and hanging open, Jasmine had no idea. "She was into local politics for a while. Lost an election or something. Empty-nester."

Jasmine nodded, happy to listen to Leah's soft, gravelly voice. It sounded the way raw brown sugar tasted, all crunch and toasted sweetness. She shook her head to clear away dangerous thoughts, relieved they'd reached the front of the line. "Two of the hot chocolates, please," she said. "And that cupcake." She pointed through the display case, her mouth already watering, desperate for the taste of the dark chocolate.

"Let's do half a dozen of the cupcakes," Leah corrected, fishing another bill out of her wallet. "Should we get a mix and match?" she asked.

Jasmine laughed, her breath exhaling in disorganized clouds of vapor. "Why so many?" she asked.

"I didn't bring anything for your family, and that's making me feel like a bad guest," Leah replied.

"You're not a bad guest, they don't expect anything from you."

"Are we doing the six?" the baker asked brightly, ready with a crisp yellow box branded with the bakery's name. Her name tag read Wren, and she beamed at both of them over the makeshift counter. "If you're not sure which other five you want, I can recommend some of our personal favorites." She pointed at a light-colored cake with a rainbow swirl of frosting. "That one is Monroe's, it's vanilla bean with raspberry and lemon frosting. And that's Jaime's, they love the carrot cake and cream cheese."

"Okay," Leah said, nodding. "What else?"

"This one is mine, it's a sponge cake. Very light, perfect with coffee, I think. Oh, and speaking of coffee, this one is new, it's a tiramisu flavor, very popular with the caffeine enthusiasts." The baker plopped each one into the box with delicate precision. "And if you have coffee, you obviously need tea, so I say we finish with the Earl Grey and lavender. It's not in season for most bakeries, but we grow all of our own botanicals in the back." She beamed proudly, folding up the box and securing it with a polka-dotted sticker. "Anything else?"

"I think we're good to go." Leah handed over the cash, tucking the box under her arm. "Can you grab my drink?"

Jasmine nodded, taking both to-go cups, grateful for the warmth. "We should drop these at the car before we get corndogs," she said. "You're going to want both hands."

Chapter Seven

Leah tossed the empty corndog sticks into the trash can, dusting crumbs from her hands. Jasmine's family hadn't been lying when they said the festival had incredible food. Prices were even reasonable for a festive fair, which was practically unheard of anymore. The hot chocolate settled into her stomach, but it wasn't enough to even get her buzzed. She'd learned back in college that her system was too quick, too efficient for that, and she couldn't afford the quantity she'd need to let loose. Still, it had been delicious, that much she couldn't deny.

"Hey," Annie said, approaching from the other side with her own empty to-go cup, this one marked with an *e* for espresso. "What have you two been up to?" she asked, craning her neck to look for Jasmine.

"She went to the bathroom," Leah answered, knowing that what Annie really wanted to know was where Jasmine was. "We've mostly been eating, although we did make it to the sculpture walk a little while ago."

Annie rubbed her palms against the cup, sapping away whatever heat was left within the thin cardboard. "And what did you think? Which was your favorite?"

"I think it's amazing what people can do with solid blocks of ice," Leah responded. "And I think the bear was my favorite."

"Oh, the bear is everyone's favorite," Annie scoffed, but she was smiling. "Who doesn't love a bear?"

"You might be surprised, actually," Leah replied, just a split second before she realized what she was saying. "I just mean, plenty of folks are afraid of bears."

"Well, none around here, thank goodness," Annie said. She skirted around the garbage can, moving closer to Leah. "I don't know how much Jazzy has told you, but... she was sick for a while. For a long time, if I'm telling the truth."

Anxiety rippled beneath Leah's skin. Her nerves were always on high alert a few days before a full moon, but lying through her teeth to a nice girl's mother was sending her off the charts into an oblivion of panic. "She did mention that, yes," Leah managed to say. "If you're worried about the cold—"

"I'm not worried about the cold, not tonight, anyway." Annie laid a hand on Leah's arm, and the pressure had a grasping, pleading quality to it. "I just want you to know that she's had a lot of complications, and it might not always be easy."

Leah rammed her hands into her pockets, wishing there had been something in them to clench in her fist. "Is anything worth doing easy?" she asked, hoping it was the correct response. "I just mean—"

Annie leaned in, her voice barely above a whisper. "Her last girlfriend left her, you know." She stopped, waiting for Leah to respond, but there wasn't anything to say, so she continued. "They were engaged, actually. She couldn't handle the possibility that Jasmine might get sick again someday. Even when she's well, there are doctor visits and checkups, and Danielle ran off, changed her phone number. I think Jazzy called it *ghosting*."

"Mom!" Jasmine hissed, pushing herself between them. "Seriously?"

"Jazzy, I'm just trying to make sure that—"

"Well, stop!" Jasmine pulled at Leah's elbow, dragging her away. "My previous illnesses aren't why Danielle moved, she was cheating on me for months with her roommate." She huffed out an angry sigh, her cheeks rosy either from the chill in the air or the rage just under the surface. "I don't think I want to be at the festival anymore, not if you're going to be harassing my girlfriend. We're going to go hitchhike home, how about that?"

Words got caught in Leah's throat, and to her horror, she wasn't saying anything, just standing there like a statue, or like some old scrap metal on the side of the road. She was a broken washing machine that fell off of someone's truck bed, dented and useless. She should have been defending Jasmine, or trying to look like a caring girlfriend, but instead, she looked like an oblivious fool. "Uh—" she managed to start.

"No, Leah, you don't have to get involved," Jasmine interrupted. "My mother does this with everyone in my life, warning them how much of a burden I might be if I get sick again."

Annie shook her head furiously, stepping towards them. "No, no, that's not what it is at all, I've told you before that I'm just trying to protect you! Sometimes, people aren't strong enough for all the nights in the hospital, for—"

"Enough, Mom," Jasmine said firmly, her fingers digging into Leah's arm, even through mittens, a thick sweater, and her leather jacket. "I'm not sick anymore."

"Jazzy, honey, I didn't mean any harm." Annie fretted with her hands, pulling at her gloved fingers, her brow creased and scrunched into a tight furrow of worry. "I just want to make sure you won't get your heart broken again."

"I, uh, don't intend on doing that," Leah said, finally, internally cursing herself for taking too long to intervene. Her words weren't even a lie—their parting, or just going back to working together, wasn't going to break Jasmine's heart. The holidays were just a business opportunity, a trade, a favor for a favor, and she'd keep repeating that to herself until she believed it. "Jasmine is stronger than you think, stronger than I am, some days, and people like being around her. Haven't you seen how easily she makes friends?" Leah adjusted her hat, despite knowing her head was sweating. "I wish I had one quarter of her confidence." She shrugged, placing a hand over Jasmine's casually, as though it was something they did every day, and not an act that sent butterflies rampaging through her stomach.

Annie stared, blinking for a moment. "That's good to hear," she said after an uncomfortable pause. "Make sure you're back at the car on time, okay Jazz? Your grandpa is already three hot chocolates deep and he's telling some teenager about the wonders of protest music."

"Yeah," Jasmine said flatly. "We'll be there."

Her mother gave Leah an apologetic wince and skulked off behind a row of food stands, tugging at her long brunette braid. "Are you okay?" Leah asked, already knowing the answer.

"I don't know, do I seem okay?" Jasmine shot back.

Leah consciously released the pressure in her shoulder blades, aware that the tension was giving her a headache. "No."

"I'm, sorry, I just—" Jasmine growled in her throat, frustrated and cloistered within the safety of her closed mouth. "I really didn't want that to happen."

"Did you think that it might?" Leah asked.

"She told college friends of mine. I was late starting, you know, because I was sick, so when I finally went I was a little older than everyone else, and only on campus part-time. It was hard to make friends when most of my classmates were fresh out of high school." Jasmine released a breath, staring up at the lights overhead. "It was better for my master's, but that was only a year, and most of it was online. The schools further downstate didn't offer what I wanted, so instead I took three trips up north to the city for my exams."

"You probably feel like you got screwed out of the quintessential college campus experience?" Leah asked gently. "I know how that feels. I only ever went part-time, night classes, trying to fit it around working at Syndicorp. Finally got my own master's a few years ago, but you know, there aren't really any jobs." She drew in a shaky breath, uncomfortable with sharing so much of herself with someone who was barely more than a stranger, even if she was starting to feel like she'd known Jasmine for years already.

Jasmine nodded. "Yeah, you just feel a bit…"

"Lost," Leah finished. "Yeah." She twisted on the spot, her boots grinding the rock salt into a fine powder. "Do you want something else to eat?"

"Nah, I think three corndogs and half a bag of popcorn was probably enough," Jasmine answered, patting her stomach through her thick coat. "Why, are you hungry?"

Leah shrugged. "I don't know, I could eat."

"What, do you have a hollow leg or something?" Jasmine asked, giggling. A snowflake, dislodged from the wire of lights above them, landed on her nose, adding a frosty white crystal to the smattering of faded freckles across her cheeks. "Thank you for that," she said earnestly. "My mom means well, she's just…"

"A lot?" Leah supplied. "And yeah, of course I wasn't going to bolt. We have an agreement, remember?"

"Still, I think most people would find that out of their jurisdiction, you know? Not within the original contract to play referee to my family drama." Jasmine scrunched up her face in embarrassment, covering her eyes with a mitten. "It's so humiliating."

"Trust me, that was nothing," Leah said. "Anyway, who doesn't have a little family theatrics around the holidays? Seems to me like it's about par for the course. Everyone dreads that part of it."

"We usually aren't like this, you know." Jasmine grabbed Leah's hand again, pulling her towards the city hall building. "I think my mom is afraid I'm going to leave."

"And are you?" Leah asked. "Leaving?"

Jasmine bit her lip, but didn't make eye contact. "I don't know. Maybe. I applied for a job at the state park downstate from here. It's an archival position, I'd be responsible for a lot of the surveyed findings over the years, for helping to manage the exhibits, that kind of thing. The pay sucks, but since when does anything ethical pay a real salary?"

Leah swallowed back a laugh, choking on it. "You're not wrong." She followed Jasmine through the throngs of people, allowing herself to be led up the steps to the small building, the doors freshly painted, but someone hadn't stripped off the old layers first. Even the handle had been painted over and was oddly slick with white paint. "What's in here?"

"Art exhibition." Jasmine pushed through the doors, sighing happily when the warmer air enveloped them both. Leah, on the other hand, was practically ready to strip off everything she was wearing to go for a swim in a snowbank. "Once we're done in here, it might be time to head back."

Leah nodded. "Okay." She twisted her arms in her sleeves, the presence of too much bulky fabric cutting off circulation to her fingers. "Sorry," she said, peeling off her coat. "I told you, I tend to run hot."

"Makes one of us," Jasmine said, and in response, Leah draped her leather jacket around Jasmine's shoulders.

"Maybe that will help with the wind, at least," she offered. "Nice photography here. Andie Zanetti." She squinted at the picture, a large black bear standing on its hind legs in a forest clearing, snow thickly blanketing the ground around it. "I wonder if that's the woman who helped you with your shutterbug tendencies outside."

"Probably," Jasmine agreed. "Lots of local artists submit to this exhibition. If they're lucky, someone with money will buy them during a visit." She turned out her empty pockets for emphasis. "Not me this year, I'm afraid."

"Mmhmm," Leah murmured, still staring at the photo. If she didn't know any better, she'd say that photographer accidentally caught a Bear on camera. As far as she knew, there weren't many in the Midwest, although there was no way to know for sure. She'd long since strayed away from the people who would know that sort of thing. Too much infighting about what Bears needed, not enough support, but when most of them were struggling to even make rent, there weren't many sources for support to come from, anyway.

"Wow, you really like bears, don't you?" Jasmine teased lightly, pulling the jacket tight around her shoulders. "Did you have a teddy bear collection as a kid?"

Leah glanced at her, unsure how to reply, of how much of herself to lay bare on the altar of fake dating. "Nah," she answered. "I just think they're cool. Did you know that when bears go after honey, they eat the bees, too?"

"Ew," Jasmine said, laughing. "Really? That sounds painful."

Leah returned the chuckle. "Oh, it is," she replied, without realizing what she'd said. "I just mean, you know, I imagine it would be. Painful. You know, to eat bees."

"Do you eat bees often?" Jasmine asked with a delicious cackle. "If you like local honey, I think I saw a stand for that near the entrance."

"Wait, seriously?" Leah asked, craning her neck to look down the path. "Have you ever tried salted honey on toast? I swear it's the nectar of the gods." She started heading towards the entrance, hunting for the booth, because despite everything she'd already eaten, she wouldn't survive the night without something else sweet, other than the cupcakes in the car. She'd leave those for Jasmine and her family. "And I don't eat bees," she added. "I did get stung a couple of times as a kid, though."

"No, I've never tried salted honey," Jasmine said, quickening her pace in order to keep up. "It was off to the left, just after that stand with all the turquoise jewelry."

Leah reached her hand out, interlacing her fingers with Jasmine's and trying not to internally panic at the contact. "I remember that one," she said, slowing down so they didn't crash into another couple, lingering under the garland of mistletoe decked between two huge pine trees, their branches weighed down with heavy, wet snow, icicles underneath sparkling the reflection of the festival. "We should probably avoid that, huh?" she asked, joking, but a part of her wishing that she wasn't.

"Looks a little crowded," Jasmine offered, tightening her grip on Leah's hand. "Hey, there's the honey," she said.

Lined up on a shelf were glass jars, each of them sporting a minimalist label with a line drawing of what kind it was. On the left, was lavender, in the center was wildflowers, and on the right, were linden, acacia, and clover varieties. Leah's mouth watered at the sight, but given the premium but fair cost, she could only afford one of them. "What's your favorite flower?" she asked.

"Oh, I don't know, I was never one for flowers," Jasmine replied. "But I do love the prairies in the summer."

"Wildflowers it is," Leah confirmed, sliding money across the counter and taking the hefty jar. "I hope you love it."

"Salted, and on toast?" Jasmine mused, burying her nose in Leah's sweater for warmth. "I can't think of anything better right now, unless it was a huge open fire." She checked her phone, frowning. "We should get to the car. Mom texted, and my grandpa is ranting and raving about the state of modern music. I'm betting he falls asleep on the drive home."

Cautiously, Leah stretched an arm out over Jasmine's shoulders, pulling her closer. She'd expected resistance but found none, and that was the most dangerous part of all.

Chapter Eight

When Jasmine awoke in her bedroom, she almost forgot that Leah was there, until she almost stepped on her after throwing off the covers. "Oh crap!" she hissed. "Sorry!"

"It's alright, it wouldn't be the first time someone has mistaken me for a rug," Leah mumbled blearily, sitting up on her makeshift sleeping bag, made of spare blankets from the linen closet and the giant rainbow pillow. She stretched her arms over her head, her hair all mussed from sleeping.

Jasmine stole a glance at her reflection and was suitably horrified. The bun she'd put her hair into was floppy and falling out, her hair sticking out at all angles, and the black liner she'd forgotten to wash off the night before smeared beneath her eyes. "I'll just be a minute," she said, willing Leah to keep her eyes closed until she was out of the room. "Small bladder, one kidney, you know."

Standing up, or trying to, her leg got caught in the sheet, and she tumbled to the ground, feeling the friction of the rug against the bare skin of her knee, mouthing silent curses.

"Are you okay?" Leah asked, still half-asleep.

"Uh huh, yup," Jasmine confirmed, wrestling her limbs from the oppressive fabric. "Be right back!"

She closed the door behind her, not wanting anyone else to see that they hadn't shared the bed. It would lead to far too many uncomfortable questions, and it would undermine the point of pretending to be together in the first place. Jasmine eased into the bathroom, locking it and staring out the window at the fresh blanket of snow, already cleared from the street in front of the house.

The water from the sink was cold, so she let it run for a few minutes to get hot before she bent to wash her face, scrubbing the previous day's makeup from her skin. She layered on two serums and a moisturizer, letting it settle before applying a new layer of makeup, eager to camouflage the dark circles under her eyes. She'd spent half the night lying awake, afraid she would snore and keep Leah up. It was already asking too much to pretend to be her girlfriend, she didn't want to keep Leah from sleeping, too.

"Jazz?" her mother called through the door, knocking softly. "Or is that you, Dad?"

"It's me, Mom," Jasmine replied through gritted teeth, still angry about the night before. She'd been grateful to just let her grandfather fill the silence with inane chatter about music and literature rather than hashing things out with her mother. "I'll be out in a minute, I'm almost done."

"Can I come in?"

Jasmine sighed, always unable to resist candid honesty. "Fine."

The brass hinges creaked in protest, and her mother sat on the edge of the tub, hands folded in her lap. "I know you're angry at me."

"Did you interrupt my morning regime just to state the obvious?" Jasmine asked acerbically, angrily blending foundation into her neck. "Yes, I'm angry. You do this, Mom, you do it every time someone new shows up, and it was already getting old five years ago. Now, it's just obnoxious."

"I don't suppose reiterating that I just want the best for you will work?" her mother asked, pulling at strands of hair that stuck out from her dark braid. "I just don't want to see you get your heart broken again."

"I'm twenty-eight, Mom."

Her mother sighed, breath catching in her throat as she wiped away a tear. "You don't have to remind me, I know."

"Danielle was a liar, and it's good that she left before anything else more serious happened." Jasmine dusted setting powder over her face before unclipping the lid of her black liquid liner. "Are you going to try to protect me from cheaters, too?"

"I would if I could, Jazz." Her mother rubbed the knees of her denim overalls as if she were trying to put holes in them. "Is Leah good to you?"

"Yeah, Mom. She's considerate." Jasmine caught her mother's eyes in the mirror and raised an eyebrow. "I hope Paps didn't mow through all those cupcakes last night. He'll have hell to pay if he ate my minty dark chocolate."

"I gave him the Earl Grey and hid the rest." Her mother cracked a smile, the clay bangles on her wrists clacking noisily. "What do you want for breakfast? Pancakes? Or we could go to that diner in town, or we could do camp potatoes and eggs, if you want."

"Leah bought some nice honey last night, maybe we can have that on toast?" Jasmine offered, immediately realizing it wasn't hers to offer. "Uh, actually, let me check on that."

"Is she awake?" her mother asked, glancing down the hallway at Jasmine's door. "Or is she more of a night owl?"

"She's awake," Jasmine replied, avoiding the rest of the question. She actually had no idea what kind of timetable Leah kept to. "Coffee?" she suggested, storing her makeup bag back in the mirrored cabinet. "Lots of coffee, maybe. You know how Paps gets after his hot chocolates."

Her mother rolled her eyes, nodding. "Oh yes, I know." She leaned out of the bathroom, cupping her hands around her mouth. "Dad!" she shouted, the sound reverberating off the ceiling's beams. "We're going to make breakfast!"

There was no reply, but that was nothing new, not for a man rarely seen before noon. "Did he fall asleep in the chair downstairs?" Jasmine asked, running a brush through her pin-straight hair, but frowning at the static. "I hate winter, I look like a vampire," she said, poking the mirror.

"You look lovely. Go ask Leah, I'm sure she'll tell you," her mother said with a wink.

"Just relax, Mom, okay? No more medical horror stories. Let's just have a nice Christmas, no reminiscing about hospital food or how good the lime gelatin was."

Her mother stood, examining the plant on the windowsill, pinching off several yellowed leaves. "I promise to behave. But if she—"

"She won't," Jasmine reiterated. "We'll be down for breakfast in a few. She might want to shower first, I'll ask her."

Padding down the short corridor, she sneaked back into her room, making sure not to open the door too widely. "Leah," she whispered, but got no response. "Leah!"

"Hmm?" Leah mumbled, rolling over. "Oh, hi. It's you."

"It's me. Are you hungry?" Jasmine asked, tugging at her quilt to straighten the bed. "Shower first?"

"What time is it?" Leah asked, squinting at the sunlight creeping in from beneath the blinds. "It looks early."

"It's eleven in the morning," Jasmine replied, teasing. "Were you planning on sleeping all day?"

"Given the opportunity." Leah sat up again, stretching out her legs. "Where did you go?"

Jasmine glanced at her as she stood at her closet, deciding what to wear. "I was freshening up."

"Not fair."

"Why isn't it fair?" she asked, incredulous.

"Most of us look like regular old mortals in the morning. You look like a ray of sunshine." She stood, yawning as she poked through her duffel bag, which she had dragged over towards the window. "What are we doing today?"

"If I know my mother, and I do, it's going to be picking a tree." Jasmine selected a shirt and laid it over her arm, reaching for a clean pair of black jeans she'd shoved in a bin at the bottom. "Are you up for that?"

"Like chopping one down? A live tree?" Leah asked, standing there in her navy blue boxers and an old band t-shirt that was so faded, Jasmine couldn't even read who it had been. Even so, she fought to avert her eyes from the curve of Leah's hips, the slender stripe of skin that peered out where the fabric didn't quite meet. "I've never done that before."

"You might have to fight my grandpa for the axe."

"The *axe*?" Leah dropped her arms to her sides, rolling her shoulders back for an impeccable posture. "What about me looks like I can handle a two-handed melee weapon?"

Jasmine shrugged easily, tossing her clothes on the bed. "I don't know, you look to me like you'd be more than fine with swinging one around." Even as she said it, she felt herself flush. She turned on the spot, not wanting to face her reflection in the mirrored doors, nor wanting to look at Leah and have her see the pink in her cheeks. "I, uh... the bathroom is free," she said. "If you want it."

"A shower sounds good," Leah said. "I was roasting last night."

"You really do run hot." Jasmine plodded towards the bathroom, plucking a large teal bath towel from the linen closet, along with a washcloth. "Let me show you how it works, it's a little fiddly," she called back to Leah. "Old house, you know." Glancing out the frosted window, the sun shone overhead, brightening the bathroom and reflecting off the pristine tiles. Her mother had been so proud that she'd regrouted them herself the past summer. "This tap is cold, this one is hot," she explained, pointing. "And for the shower, you lift this part here." She demonstrated, sending a spray of cold water against the shower curtain, printed with large tropical leaves.

"Great," Leah said, yawning as she ran a hand through her hair, brushing back the longer bits in the front and tucking them behind her ear, which sported three simple silver hoops through the cartilage. "I promise not to take too long."

"I'd be impressed if you took longer than ten minutes, because that's usually when the boiler runs out," Jasmine said with a laugh. "Do you need anything else? Soap, shampoo?"

"I brought my own." Leah lifted the small grey plastic caddy stuffed with bath products. "Sensitive skin."

"Oh," Jasmine replied. "Me too." She turned off the faucet and pulled back the shower curtain, revealing the same products on her shelf. "It's good, right?"

"Yeah, the only thing that doesn't make me break out," Leah agreed. "What time are we leaving?"

Jasmine shrugged, checking her watch. "Whenever we're all ready, I would guess. I heard my mom shower this morning, and my grandpa probably won't until later."

"So we're all waiting on me?" Leah asked, setting the caddy on the side of the tub and hanging the fresh towel on the rail.

"Yeah, but you're worth the wait." Jasmine bit her lip, unsure if that was overstepping whatever unseen boundary line was between them for the weekend. Leah smiled, glowing for just a second before she reset her face to a neutral expression.

"I mean, it sounds like you're going to need some muscle out there today. Chopping down a whole tree? Who does that these days?" She rested her hand against the sink, leaning gently so that her oversized band t-shirt clung to her muscular frame.

Jasmine raised a quizzical eyebrow. "Plenty of people, Erickson. Just wait, I'll make you a live-tree convert." She stepped outside the bathroom, even though a small, greedy part of her wanted to stay, to sit in the steam and talk, to catch a glimpse of those abs, too—she shook her head, tugging at her pajamas. "We'll be downstairs. Oh, do you mind if I try some of that honey you bought?"

"I mean, I bought it for you, so... yeah." Leah averted her eyes, turning her attention back to the taps. "Thanks for the tutorial."

"Sure, yeah, any time," Jasmine offered, latching the door. After a second, she heard the lock click into place. "Geeze, Jazz, way to make it weird," she mumbled to herself.

Picking through her closet, she wasn't quite sure why she was feeling hostile towards everything hanging there. None of it looked right on her, it all just hung off her, or was too snug in one place and not in another, or had a stain she'd missed in the laundry. She groaned aloud, flicking her way through the hangers for a third time. "Jazzy," her mother called from the bottom of the stairs. "Are you coming down, or what?"

"Yeah, I'm getting dressed," she shouted back. "Can't find anything to wear."

"You have those other jeans in the laundry room," her mother supplied. "And I think that red plaid just came out of the tumble dryer, the padded one with the fleece."

Jasmine was halfway down the stairs three seconds later, taking the steps two at a time. "Thanks, Mom," she said hastily, rushing past her through the kitchen and into the garage. As promised, jeans and a warm shirt, perfect for tree-hunting. She hopped from one foot to the other, the cold concrete immediately biting through her knitted socks into the soles of her feet, chilling her to the bone. The glass of water her grandpa had left there the night before was frosted along the surface, the fractals perfectly even. Jasmine almost hated to ruin them by taking it inside, but if she didn't, there would be broken glass by the next morning.

"There you are," her mother said, forearms pressed against the island. "Breakfast?"

"Yeah, I'm starved," Jasmine replied, finishing the buttons on her shirt before closing the garage door. "Cold out there today."

Her mother nodded, the dark braid at her shoulder reaching almost to her waist with a stripe of grey just at the front. It hadn't been there before Jasmine had gotten sick. "The forecast said there might be a blizzard soon."

"Today?"

"No, in a few days, but they said it might pass over us. You know how these things are," her mother said with a shrug. "You ready for tree-hunting?"

Jasmine dropped two slices of bread into the old toaster and depressed the lever, her stomach already growling. "I'm always ready," she replied. "Leah has never been, so maybe take it easy on her."

"Who isn't taking it easy?" her mother asked, defensive, her arms now folded over her chest. "Honestly, Jazzy, you think that I—"

"Mom," Jasmine warned. "Last night—"

Her mother interrupted her with a resigned sigh, letting her arms fall back to her sides. "Alright, alright, I hear you," she relented. "I won't give her a hard time. If you want, Paps can do the chopping. I know you don't like risking sap in your hair."

"A mistake I made once, and never will again," Jasmine reiterated. "A lesson very quickly learned, even if I was only twelve." The toaster popped, and she retrieved the two slices, dropping them onto a plate. Digging through her messenger back that was hanging off the back of a stool, she located the honey, sliding it across the counter. "Leah said she got this for me to try."

"Wildflowers," her mother read aloud. "Sounds nice. Mind if I try some?"

"Leah said it's good with salt." Jasmine fetched a flat knife from the drawer, ready to spread the sticky goodness across the crispy bread. The smell itself was enough to stimulate a ravenous hunger within her, something almost feral, and it was just honey and bread, something so simple.

"No salt for you," her mother chided. "You know you have to watch your intake."

"One more word and I'm not letting you have any honey," Jasmine said, snatching the jar back. "Promise me you'll stop, just for a few days."

"Fine," her mother said, her tone clipped and curt. "I'll stop."

Chapter Nine

Leah bent over, scrubbing the water out of her hair with the plush towel. It smelled like lavender and chamomile, soothing and soft. She made a mental note to change her fabric softener, because it sure as heck wasn't doing its job. Tugging on her boxers, she let the elastic snap around her narrow hips as she wiped rivulets of condensation from the mirror.

She dressed quickly, her favorite blue jeans, a black t-shirt, and the green plaid that she'd taken from the closet earlier that morning. It had been tempting to poke through Jasmine's clothes, but she'd resisted the impulse, even as her fingertips grazed against the brushed cotton. Thick socks, because even if she ran hot, improper socks with boots always felt gross to her.

Before running down the stairs, she glanced at her reflection, frowning at her hair. She'd have to try yet another barber in the hopes they'd cut it the way she wanted. For the moment, she ruffled it with her hands, aiming for a lightly unkempt look, a little bit scruffy and endearing, and then wondered why she cared so much in the first place, seeing as it was just a ruse for the holidays.

"Morning," she said, bounding down the stairs, landing heavily at the base. "Sorry if I took too long."

"Nonsense!" Annie protested, appearing in the kitchen doorway. "Jazzy is just trying out some of that honey you got from the festival last night." She cast a skeptical glance up the stairs, narrowing her eyes. "Any sign of my dad?"

"Still sleeping, I would guess," Leah answered. "Not a peep."

"Dad!" Annie protested. "If you don't get up right now, we're leaving without you and we all know you have strong opinions about the tree!"

Upstairs, the far door creaked open, and there was the sound of shuffling slippers. "I'm up, I'm up," he grumbled. "Heaven forfend we be late to an activity with no time limit."

"The best ones will all be gone by three," Annie shouted back. "Do you want another sad excuse of a tree like two years ago? That thing dropped so many needles, there was nothing left but the trunk and a few spindly branches by Christmas day."

Martin sighed, pausing at the top of the stairs. "You're never going to let that go, are you?"

Annie shook her head. "So hurry up." She waited until he was in the bathroom to turn back towards the kitchen, hands cupped around a festive mug shaped like a bear and adorned with ceramic trees and lights.

"You like bears?" Leah asked, nodding at it. "It's cute."

"I love bears," Annie replied, holding the mug out for inspection. "Jazz does, too. I think she had about a hundred teddy bears at one point." She pulled it back to her chest, taking a sip. "Coffee?"

"Perfect." Leah followed her into the kitchen, sitting next to Jasmine at the island. "Morning," she said, nudging her shoulder. "I like your shirt."

Annie poured out a mug of steaming coffee. "Milk? Sugar?" she asked, hand hovering over a teaspoon.

"Both," Leah answered. "Thanks."

"Oh, look!" Annie exclaimed, sliding a mug shaped like a snowperson across the tiles. "Jazzy is in red, and Leah, you're in green. Together, you're perfectly festive!"

"Yeah, we planned that," Jasmine lied, finishing up the last of her toast. "Damn, that honey was good. Thank you, Leah."

"Did you try it with salt?" Leah asked, sipping at the coffee. She wasn't cold, but it warmed something previously unreachable within her, like a stubborn icicle when spring was trying to burst forth.

Jasmine exchanged a look with her mother and shrugged. "A little," she replied. "I don't think it needs much."

"Nah, just a little," Leah agreed. "I might grab some if you don't mind." She stood, stepping towards the bread box on the counter, the pine wood bright in the morning sunshine.

Annie intercepted the bread, blocking the counter before Leah could get there. "Nonsense," she said. "I'll do it. You're our guest!" She took out two slices and dropped them into the toaster, facing the tiled backsplash. "I will revise my position if you're ever more than a guest here. You know, if you're a more... permanent fixture?"

"Mom!" Jasmine interjected. "I told you not to scare her off."

"Oh, I don't know," Leah said, locking eyes with Jasmine and feeling terrified about it, "I'm not that easily scared off."

"I, uh..." Jasmine trailed off, clearing her throat. "Yeah. Yes. Good. See, Mom? No need for weird veiled comments." She tore her eyes away, looking down at the remaining crumbs on her plate.

Leah took it, brushing the crumbs into the garbage, prepared to reuse it for her breakfast. She was desperate for the topic to shift, for something to draw attention away from her reddening cheeks because she was finding it increasingly more difficult to separate the fact from the fiction of her feelings about Jasmine. The story was they'd been dating for three months. The truth was that after Christmas, they'd go back to being coworkers and nothing more. As much as Leah disliked the season, she didn't want Christmas to be over. Dread had already settled into her stomach, the hours ticking by too eagerly as she tried to cling to the fairytale.

"Here's your toast," Annie said, dropping the slices onto the plate. "Honey is on the island near Jazzy. She pointed at the salt grinder next to the stove. "And the salt is there, if you feel you need it." There was a strange pointedness to her tone that Leah couldn't quite figure out, but she knew she had to tread lightly.

"So, tree-hunting?" she asked, turning to slather a thick layer of honey onto the brown toast. "I've never been."

"Never?" Annie demanded, astonished. "You never cut down a tree?"

"I mean, I've chopped wood for stoves and that kind of stuff, but I've never gone after a live tree." Leah left the salt shaker where it was, unsure of why it was an issue, but very sure she didn't want to reintroduce the matter. "My family wasn't that big on the holidays growing up."

Annie refilled her bear mug from the coffee pot, leaving just enough for one more cup. "Why is that?"

"Uh, kind of a broken home situation," Leah answered, surprising even herself with her honesty. "It just wasn't ever a priority along with everything else."

"So no tree?" Annie asked, dropping three sugar cubes into her coffee. "No lights, or presents or anything? No stockings?"

Leah crammed a whole slice in her mouth, hoping for the extra time to figure out her response. "Not really," she replied through a mouthful of toast and sweet, summery honey. She did miss the salt, but not enough to test Annie's boundaries on the matter. "But it's okay, I don't really go for all the commercialism anyway. It's all kind of a lot."

"We don't go too wild," Jasmine reassured her, laying a hand on Leah's arm. "It's mostly about the food, anyway."

Despite the toast, Leah's stomach growled angrily. She'd need a couple of granola bars if they were going to be out tromping through the snow, dragging a helpless tree back to the car. "Food is good," she said, with an undercurrent of desperation to keep the conversation moving, and not lingering on her past. "What's on the menu for this year?"

"Oh, a smörgåsbord," Martin announced, adjusting his knitted sweater, the stitches bulky but even, the cables twisting neatly up to the ribbed collar. "We've got a whole freezer full of goodies outside. Ham, turkey, potatoes—" His face drained of all its color. "Annie. The ham. The turkey. I never took them out to defrost."

"I got it, Paps," Jasmine said, opening the refrigerator to show him it had already been done, both items sitting inside aluminum roasting trays on the center shelf. "Took them out yesterday."

Martin beamed at his granddaughter, pulling his daughter in for a sideways hug as he tried to steal her coffee. "It's a Christmas miracle!" he shouted. "The holiday is saved!"

"We don't have to be so theatrical, Dad," Annie said, shoving an empty mug into his hands. "And you can get your own coffee. You don't even like mine, you think it's too sweet."

"Tis the season for theatrics," he countered, pouring the last of the coffee into his mug along with a healthy splash of milk from the ceramic carafe on the counter. "Why do you think everyone goes out to see A Christmas Carol, or The Nutcracker this time of year?"

"Paps, The Nutcracker is a ballet," Jasmine said with a snort.

"Maybe so, but it still requires the artistry of the theater. I once played Ebeneezer Scrooge in a production, I'll have you know." He leaned against the island, sipping his coffee. "I remember the lines like it was yesterday."

"So you like theater?" Leah asked, already finished with the second slice of toast. That close to a full moon, she was practically voracious. "Do you still audition?"

"He was in that production in nineteen-sixty-four," Annie answered for him, adjusting the length of her overall straps with one hand. "And nothing since."

"I appreciate the arts!" Martin argued. "I just have other things to concern myself with now. I'm a very busy man in retirement, I'll have you all know. I'm booked solid in the new year. Not a single day free until May."

"Booked solid with that easy chair in the living room, maybe," Jasmine countered. "It's fine, Paps, you don't have to go and climb a mountain to prove yourself. You'd be hard-pressed in the Midwest, anyway."

Martin scoffed, the corners of his mouth turned upwards into a smile. "There is one mountain a few hours north, actually. I think there's a ski lodge there. I went, once, about twenty years ago." He puffed out his cheeks with a dramatic sigh. "The years don't stop, do they?" He drained his mug, rinsing it in the sink before he placed it in the rack. "I'm ready, who else?"

"I need something from upstairs," Leah said quickly, already moving out of the kitchen. She already needed some extra energy, her temples had already started with a dull, pulsing throb.

"I'll get it," Jasmine offered, skating past her by sliding on the hardwood in her socks. "If we let him start crowing about anything else, we'll never get out of here."

"Well, excuse me for trying to keep the conversation moving," Martin said, pretending to be offended, holding a hand to his chest in mock defiance. "A man only wants to make polite small talk, you know."

"No, no," Leah protested, edging past her on the stairs. "I don't mind."

"What, are you hiding something?" Jasmine teased, but her face fell when Leah didn't immediately object. She followed Leah into the bedroom, pushing the door to the frame. "*Are* you hiding something?"

Leah poked at her bag with her toe. "It's nothing weird," she mumbled.

"Then what is it?"

"Protein bars?" Leah unzipped the duffel, showing the stash of wrapped snacks tucked into the side, just behind three rolled-up t-shirts.

Jasmine shook her head, laughing. "Why are you being cagey about protein bars?" she asked. "Are you trying to bulk up or something? Because I have to tell you, you don't need all that. You already look—" she coughed, trying to cover what she'd said.

"I already look what?" Leah asked, torn between being desperate to hear the answer and never wanting to know. "How do I look?" she pressed after a silence, pocketing three of the protein bars, shoving them down deep into her pockets. "What do I look like?"

"Good," Jasmine said after a moment. "That's all I was going to say. You look good." She shrugged, but there was an air of petulance to it, like she'd been caught with her hand in the cookie jar.

"It's okay, you don't have to say that," Leah replied. "And no, that's not why. I just have a fast metabolism. I get hungry."

Jasmine's shoulders relaxed, and she sat on the bed, hands on her knees. "Oh. You're allowed to eat, you know. You can just go foraging in the fridge, no one is going to say anything."

"I'd rather not risk it." Leah zipped up her duffel again, shoving it back underneath the bed. "There's already stuff in there for Christmas, and I wouldn't want to accidentally eat it. It's fine, I came prepared." She patted her pockets with a telltale crunch, standing up straight again.

"Leah—" Jasmine started, cutting herself off, chewing on her lip. "Leah, if you're into anything weird, I'd rather you just told me now."

"It's a protein bar, not contraband, Jasmine," Leah shot back. She hadn't anticipated being accused of doing anything illegal, but her insecurity about the snack was exactly why she'd wanted to retrieve them herself. It was also why she'd spent most of her time alone. People didn't understand even the tiniest minutiae of what she was, and none of them had ever wanted to find out. "If you want, I can just leave now."

"What?" Jasmine said, shaking her head emphatically. "No! No, I don't want you to go," she whispered. "I just don't like surprises."

Doubt and shame twisted like a knife in Leah's gut, threatening to void her breakfast out onto the rug. She swallowed back the bile and folded her arms over her chest, more a motion of protection than anything else. "I didn't realize a protein bar would be a surprise," she said evenly, knowing that if a snack caused that much of a problem, she'd never be able to be truly honest with Jasmine, and maybe that was for the best. She'd been a fool to think otherwise, and internally vowed not to lose sight of what was at stake. If Jasmine didn't cover those shifts, Leah would get fired, and without any savings, she'd be in serious financial trouble pretty much immediately.

"It's not, I just didn't understand why you were being cagey about it. I thought it might have, like, steroids or something." Jasmine pulled at the cuffs of her shirt, fraying the worn threads there.

"You think they put steroids into protein bars?" Leah crossed to the closet, yanking her leather jacket off the hanger and leaving the hat on the shelf. "You think I'm on steroids?"

"I mean, you are pretty muscular," Jasmine offered, shrugging her shoulders. She tried for a grin, but it landed lopsided on her cheeks. "I'm sorry, Leah. I don't want you to go, okay? I just—I don't like not having control over a situation. I spent too long like that when I was sick, you know?"

Leah sighed, feeling some of the irritation melt off of her and sink into the wood floor, the panels creaking beneath her feet. "Yeah, okay, I understand," she relented. "I'm not on steroids. They are just protein bars. I get really hungry, and some people are weird about that, so I usually prefer to hide that."

"You can tell me when you're hungry. We're not weird about food in this house." Jasmine bit her lip for a second, and then released it, the fullness a tempting reddish pink. "Not like that, anyway."

"I will tell you if I am hungry," Leah lied, already intending to stick to her plan. Most people didn't understand just how hungry a Bear could get near and during a full moon. It wasn't unusual to eat three or four times as much as she usually did. "Shall we go murder a tree?"

"Yes," Jasmine said, taking her arm. "Let's."

Chapter Ten

The Frostlake Reserve was huge, spanning hundreds of acres of trees and dormant prairies just waiting for spring to awaken them once more. Pine trees pressed up into the horizon, their spiny tips stationary even in the light breeze. They had always been Jasmine's favorites, so stoic and serene, always dependable and constant. Despite the frustrations of that morning, she breathed deep the scent of conifers, bracing in its complexity.

"Well, this is it," she said, taking a small axe from the trunk of their station wagon. "Are you ready?"

Leah nodded, taking in the landscape. "As ready as I'll ever be, I guess."

"Who wants to sing carols?" Jasmine's grandfather asked, throwing an arm each around his daughter and granddaughter. "I'll start us off. Jolly good king—"

"Dad!" Jasmine's mother protested with a laugh. "No one wants to sing!"

He made the motion of zipping his mouth shut with an apologetic bow. "My deepest apologies, ladies," he said. "I was overtaken by the festive spirit." He marched up to the gate, no more than a low wooden fence, gesturing back to the rest of them. "Hello, my good man!" he started. "We're here for a tree. All four of us. Four, in total. One tree."

The attendant pointed out towards the tree line in the distance, probably a third of a mile through the snow. "On the left are the mature trees, they're all labeled with colored rings." He gestured to a sign indicating the prices for each species. "On the right are the babies, we ask that if you want a smaller tree that you accept one that we choose. We have a strong policy of conservation here.”

“Nah, not for me,” her grandfather said. “The bigger the better. Six-foot minimum.”

“Maximum,” Annie corrected. “It won’t fit in the house, otherwise.” She took a flyer from the attendant, reading over the prices. “Don’t listen to my father, he’s been overtaken by the ghost of Christmas present, apparently.” She eyed the horizon, already looking for the perfect tree. “Many left?” she asked.

“Not a huge selection, but plenty of healthy specimens,” the attendant replied. “You may have to settle for a different kind than you usually get.”

“I don’t want a dorky-looking tree,” her mother reiterated. “I want it to be nice and full.”

The attendant nodded, staring past her. “I don’t think you’ll have any trouble there, ma’am, but we do close in an hour.”

Jasmine’s mother turned and pointed at her father. “See? I told you we needed to leave earlier. Now we only have an hour to find the perfect tree, chop it down, and get it tied to the roof rack.”

“Relax, Annie,” he said. “That’s plenty of time. Right, Leah?”

“Uh, yeah, absolutely,” Leah assured him, resting the axe on her shoulder. “Tree murder, let’s do it.”

“Each tree is replaced with two more,” the attendant corrected. “And all the funds raised go to support this reserve. It’s the only one in three counties, you know.”

Something flashed across Leah’s face, but she nodded. “Yeah, I know.”

Jasmine pushed past all of them through the gate, letting it swing back in the other direction as she released it. “While you three are yammering away about how little time we have, I’m going to find a tree.” She strode past several other families dragging trussed trees back from the woods, a few of them looking like they’d had the argument of their lives beyond the numerous pines. One kid looked half-frozen, stumbling back to the car with cold feet and bad boots.

“Hold on there, missy,” her mother said, jogging to catch up, the dense snow crunching pleasantly under her boots. “Since when do you decide which tree is the best?"

"When you two decided to spend five minutes out of our precious hour lollygagging." She smirked, shoving her hands into her pockets. "I'm not leaving here without a tree, so unless you want Leah and me to make all the decisions, you should probably get the lead out."

"If you and Leah want to make all the decisions, then I strongly suggest you get your own tree," her mother retorted, swinging her arms wildly to balance in the deep snow, the edges of her long parka dragging along the surface. "We all know I choose the best trees."

Her grandfather laughed heartily, holding his stomach as he braced against the gate. "Oh, come on now, Annie," he wheezed, "don't you remember last year's tree? The trunk was so crooked, I don't think that thing was ever straight."

Leah threw off a casual shrug. "Same."

Jasmine bent double with laughter, grabbing onto Leah so that she didn't fall over, head-first into the wet snow. "Same!" she repeated. "Oh, my God, same."

Her mother took the lead, heading further across the field, stepping down into a better-worn path, made by other tree-hunters over the past several weeks. "If you three are done making jokes, maybe we can get started," she said, still laughing herself. "And Dad, you don't have room to talk. Neither do you, Jazz."

"What?" Jasmine asked, incredulous. "What did I ever do?"

"Three years ago, that tree you insisted would fit in the front room, but it was about eighteen inches too tall? We had to give it a buzz-cut!"

Jasmine followed onto the path, quickly catching up to her mother and pulling on her elbow. "Um, I think you might remember that it was a stylistic choice to cut the top off, Mom. It was all the rage in the magazines that year."

Her mother cast her a skeptical look from the corner of her eye. "Yeah, sure, we can pretend that was the story."

Leah hopped out in front, axe resting on her shoulder like she cut down trees every day. In an odd way, it suited her, all black leather and zippers and green plaid sticking out at the bottom. It was certainly a different look than she had at work, in endless pairs of black jeans paired with those ugly grey vests. She was pensive, but not standoffish like Jasmine had thought. Truth be told, she hadn't expected her to agree to the gambit. It was so ridiculous, and yet it had been strange how easily the conversation flowed with her around.

"There are some nice ones back that way," Leah said, pointing off to the left. "Behind the first row, those take all the wind damage. You want one that's a little more sheltered."

"For someone who's never done this before, you sure have a lot of good instincts," Jasmine's grandfather offered, walking only slightly behind. "Maybe this is your calling."

Leah left the path, sinking deep into the snow, almost past the lip of her boots. "I've just spent a lot of time in these woods."

"What?" Jasmine said. "Why didn't you say?"

"Wasn't sure it was the same place until we pulled up." Leah swerved around one tree, bending to look at another. "Nah. This one is dropping too many needles."

"You see, Dad?" Jasmine's mother chided. "I told you all the good ones would be gone if we waited this far into the month. But no, you wanted to keep to tradition."

"There's nothing wrong with having a tradition," he argued, pulling the plaid hat further down over his ears. "It's just that a lot of people these days think that tradition means something else entirely."

Leah reached through the branches of another tree, shaking it. "What about this one?" she suggested, showing off that not many needles had fallen from its limbs.

"Too tall," Jasmine replied, standing next to it to estimate its height. "It shouldn't be more than a few inches taller than me. Trust me."

A frigid breeze blew through the trees, chilling her despite the bright sunshine overhead. Icicles hung from the immature trees on the other side of the path, weighing heavily on the young branches. It was a baptism of ice—either those trees would survive the winter and become stronger, or they would fail and be turned into mulch come spring. Jasmine wondered how long until she herself became no more than mulch. Life hadn't turned out the way she'd hoped it would.

"Aha!" her mother shouted, triumphant in her discovery. "This is it. The perfect tree. Pack it in, all of you, we aren't going to find anything better than this."

Jasmine turned, ready to inspect the tree, and found herself swallowing back a choked laugh. "Mom, the back side of that tree is basically completely bare."

"We can have that side facing the wall!" she argued. "It's perfect when you think about it. We wouldn't even need as many lights."

"Is that supposed to be a benefit?" Jasmine asked. "The lights are the best part!"

Her grandfather nodded, his hand grasping another tree. "I think you'll find this is the best tree," he announced. "Look at it, it couldn't be better."

"Paps, it's three feet tall," Jasmine countered. "I don't think that's even supposed to be on this side. It probably grew by accident."

He maintained his grip on the tree, still adamant. "Well, all the best things happen by accident," he countered. "I met your grandmother by accident. I got my first job by accident. Heck, I chose the paint color for the living room by accident!"

"It's a nice dark green," Leah agreed, still picking her way through the nursery of trees. "I have to admit, it's a good choice for a room that gets so much light. Calming." She turned, appraising the tree with a keen eye. "Jazz is right, though. It's too short."

"You know, Jazzy, I never would have suggested you invite your girlfriend for the holidays if I'd known you two were going to gang up on me." He huffed out an indignant sigh, finally releasing the small tree. "I'm coming back for you next year," he instructed, picking an icicle from the top. "You will be mine."

"Hey," Leah whispered, standing next to a tall, full tree, the needles a frosted green. "What about this one?"

Jasmine inspected it, finding a clean, straight trunk. "Shake it," she instructed. Leah did as she requested, but hardly any needles fell to the ground. "What does the back look like?"

"Decent," Leah said, moving out of the way so that Jasmine could look for herself. "Better than the one your mom found, anyway."

"She hates the cold, she just wants to get coffee from that stand to warm up her hands," Jasmine replied quietly. "That woman would lay in the sun every day, given half an opportunity."

The back of the tree was almost as full as the front, the difference being negligible. Jasmine held out her arms to casually measure width and height, nodding. "I think this might be it, Erickson."

"Really?" Leah beamed with pride, resting the head of the axe on the toe of her boot.

"Yeah, how did you find it?" Jasmine asked. "And what do you mean you spend a lot of time out here? You never mentioned it once to me, not even when we were going over stuff at the cafe. In fact, I think you barely told me anything there!"

The smile faded from Leah's face, and she turned towards another tree, poking at the needles with her bare fingers. "It's a long story, and not very interesting."

"Do you like hiking or something?" Jasmine kept a hand on their tree, making sure it stayed theirs, despite the lack of any other people in their vicinity.

"Or something," Leah confirmed. "Listen, I'm sorry I mentioned it, I should have kept quiet. This project is for you, not for me, that's why I didn't tell you everything. There's a lot that you don't need to know. It's not relevant."

"Why are you being so secretive? What is it really that you're hiding?" Jasmine demanded. "First furtive protein bars, now secrets about woodland hiking? What's going on with you?"

"Hey!" her grandfather shouted from two rows away. "Annie, it looks like the girls found something!"

"Nothing is going on," Leah hissed. "Over here!" she shouted, returning a hand to the trunk. "Jasmine found a good one!"

"What do you mean I found it, you clearly—"

"It's nice and tall!" Leah continued, interrupting her. "Full, too."

Jasmine's mother and grandpa gathered around the fir, nodding appreciatively. "I think it looks great," her mother agreed. "Leah, do you want to do the honors?"

Leah removed her jacket, hanging it from the branch of a neighboring tree. "I can give it my best shot." She bent, inspecting the trunk of the tree, feeling along the bark with her hands. "I'll try to get as even a cut as I can, but we might need to even it out with a hand saw or something." She glanced up at Jasmine's grandfather, who nodded.

"We've got that," he confirmed. "Let er' rip."

With a solemn nod, Leah squared her shoulders, her biceps bulging out against the cotton fabric of her shirt as she raised the axe to the appropriate level. She swung, landing a solid blow in the center of the trunk with a sharp crack that echoed out over the bare snow, but deadened in the woods.

Jasmine couldn't help but watch her as she swung twice more, the tree already beginning to give way. Leah was strong, stronger than Jasmine had realized. The axe sailed out over the brisk air with ease, dangerous but controlled. She looked as though she'd been doing that her entire life, the blade an extension of her arm. Leah sank the hatchet into the trunk once more, severing it from the stump.

"Damn," Jasmine whispered under her breath. She cleared her throat, hoping she hadn't been heard. "Nicely done," she said aloud. "Very efficient. Are you sure you've never done this before?"

"Not at that angle," Leah replied. "But my family had a wood stove when I was growing up. Chopping wood was the least boring chore. I got lucky that my brother hated it, he never fought me on a trade." She straightened, retrieving her jacket. "Watch it, there's sap on the handle."

"I'm going to bring you every year, because I can't stand sap," Jasmine said, before realizing exactly which words had escaped her mouth in the wrong order. "I just mean, good job."

"You never know, Leah might wind up here next year," Jasmine's grandfather offered, giving the tree a vigorous shake to dislodge anything that may have been living in there. "This went much faster with an experienced pair of hands."

"I don't know about experienced," Leah said. "But I'm glad to help however I can."

It didn't escape Jasmine's notice that Leah hadn't said anything about the next year comment, and while a part of her was grateful that she'd glossed over it, there was a dangerously growing part of her that wished their little charade was the truth.

"So, no residents?" Jasmine asked, nodding at the tree. "If not, we should get back to the car. I know Mom needs a coffee before she turns into an ice cube."

"Me, what about you?" her mother argued. "You must be half-frozen already! Here, let me give you my scarf—"

Leah draped her jacket around Jasmine's shoulders again. "I'm a bit warm, actually. Fast metabolism."

"No wonder you're good at this, you have ice in your veins," Jasmine replied, secretly grateful both for the jacket and for the intervention of her mother's casual overbearance. "If I didn't know any better, I'd say you were part polar bear."

"Nah," Leah said, still carrying the axe. "My mother's side is grizzly, actually."

"Mom jokes?" Jasmine's mother protested. "You two are making mom jokes? You know, Leah, I bet your mom wouldn't appreciate that too much. Maybe if I meet her someday I'll tell her that little quip about being grizzled."

Leah's step faltered, but only for a second. "I doubt that's going to happen, Annie," was all she said.

Panic climbed up Jasmine's legs, lodging in the stiffness of her knees as she fought to free her boot from the snow. "She just means that her family lives out on the coast," she interjected. "That's all."

"Yeah," Leah agreed, gratefully taking the out that Jasmine had provided. "They live out on the east coast, where I grew up. They don't come out here this much, you know, flyover states or whatever."

"That's a shame they don't want to make the effort to come out here to see you," Jasmine's mother said softly. "I know you've only been hanging around us for a couple of days, but I'd say you were worth the drive."

Leah hesitated, almost tripping over the compacted snow at the edges of the path. "Oh," she said. "I should have said it before, but thank you for inviting me."

"No girlfriend of my daughter is going to spend Christmas alone. Hey, Dad, where do you think you're taking that tree? The gate is in the other direction if you—no, I *am* sure, just look where you're going!" Jasmine's mother trudged after him, ready to rescue the perfect tree from getting dragged any further up the wrong path.

The sun was hanging low in the sky already, the sunset unusually brilliant for a winter's day near the solstice. Jasmine reached out, taking Leah's hand in her own, offering comfort because she didn't know what else to say.

"I'm sorry," Leah said quietly. "I wasn't thinking. I didn't mean it like that." She squeezed Jasmine's hand, brushing a thumb over the pilled knitting of the mitten. "I told you, I'm just not that close with them."

"Big blowout?" Jasmine asked, cautious because she could feel the palpable desire to flee rolling off of Leah in waves. "A fight? Was it about, you know, liking women?"

Leah exhaled a laugh through her nose. "I don't even think they know. They never knew me, not really, and didn't care to find out." She inhaled deeply, relaxing her shoulders until they were back to their usual placement, instead of high and tight around her ears. "It's not some big trauma, we just don't bother with each other. They're all pretty wrapped up with their own lives."

"I know what you mean. I've only seen Damien once since the surgery. It doesn't bother me so much, but Mom..." she trailed off, hanging back from her family. "Mom never really got over it."

"I caught that." Leah laid an arm around Jasmine's shoulders, pulling her closer even though neither member of her family was looking back at them. "So, it's a pretty good tree, right?"

"Yeah," Jasmine agreed, leaning into the embrace. "It's a damned good tree."

Chapter Eleven

The tree was regal and majestic already, despite it still being bare. They'd moved it to where the large bay window in the living room was, so that you could see it from the street. Leah volunteered to bring the boxes up from their basement, dodging at least three huge spiders that she'd disturbed.

"Is that all of them?" she asked, ascending the final few stairs with a clear plastic box, adorned with a bright red snap lid. "Or is there something else down there?"

"No, I reckon that's all of it," Martin said, prying the lid off of the first box she'd dropped on the floor near the tree. "Annie, this one is the lights. They look tangled."

"They're always tangled, Dad," Annie said, peering into the abyss of green cords and black plugs. "Weren't you the one who told me that little gremlins break into the boxes during the year to knot up the cords, just to make our lives difficult?"

Martin raised an eyebrow before moving to the next box. "Yes, well, I'd hoped they would have moved out by now." He pulled another lid off, kneeling down beside it. "Jazz, this one has Halloween stuff in it. Why does it have a red lid?"

"Red and orange look pretty similar in the basement when you're trying to get the heck out of there as soon as possible," Jasmine said, defending herself. "Have you seen the size of the spiders down there?"

"Maybe next year you can put them to work as Halloween decorations," Leah suggested, perching at the edge of the overstuffed wingback chair.

"Make those spiders pay rent."

"Rent is a scam," Martin grumbled, picking up a third box. "I think these are the ornaments," he said. "Jazz, do you want to do the honors?"

"Of course, fine sir," Jasmine replied, ripping the lid off the box. "Yup, it's ornaments." She set it in the center of the living room, taking each one out and unwrapping it from its paper towel packaging. A small felted donkey, a surfing Santa, and two sparkling green pickles. "Leah, can I put you on lights duty?" she asked without looking up.

Leah nodded, already accepting a ball of tangled nonsense from Annie, who was all too gleeful to pass it off. "Sure, leave it to me."

"Lights go first," Martin asserted. "Then garlands, then ornaments. Leah, no pressure, but we're all waiting on you." He sat back on his haunches, pointedly staring before he barked out a laugh. "I'm just kidding you. Here, toss me an end. I bet it's not as bad as it looks."

"You're right, it's worse," Jasmine said, picking up another compacted lump of lights, this one with fat, vintage-style bulbs in a rainbow of colors.

Martin reached for it, taking the bundle into his arms like a baby. "These remind me of the tree your grandmother and I used to put up," he said. "You should have seen the tree we had our first year together. She was pregnant with you, Annie, too big to get the lights around the tree herself. I came home from work and she was crying on the sofa because she'd wanted to surprise me." A tear gathered in the corner of his eye, but he brushed it away before it could cascade down his leathered cheeks. "So we did it together and ate Chinese takeout on the living room floor."

"Hey, let's use these lights this year," Jasmine said gently, taking the tangle from him. "Leah, maybe you can help me?"

"Of course." Leah sat on the floor, across the box from Jasmine, methodically weaving bits of wire back and forth, the edges growing with every pass. "I like these lights. They have a nice appeal to them."

"Everyone has the same damned lights these days," Martin said, emotion clouding his voice. "Tiny warm white lights and never anything different. Would you believe the latest House and Yard magazine said that multi-colored lights are *tacky?*"

Leah pulled the plug free from the center of the ball, a considerable victory given how bad the knots were. "The only thing that's tacky about trees is people judging them," she said, tugging on another bulb, this one orange. "I can't stand people like that. And besides, all those curated trees are boring. I say, the weirder, the better."

"Careful, you're going to encourage him," Jasmine teased, freeing a blue bulb from the mess. "Next thing you know he's going to be pulling out the old photo albums."

"Don't tempt me," Martin said. "I would love the opportunity to show your shiny new girlfriend your deeply embarrassing old baby photos." He leaned forward on the sofa, talking in a conspiratorial stage whisper. "Meet me in the kitchen at midnight, Leah, if you want to see them. I promise you won't be disappointed, there's one of her at age three and a half screaming bloody murder on Santa's lap."

"Hey, I maintain that mall Santa had sketchy vibes," Jasmine retorted, pointing at him. "He smelled like stale beer and dead dreams."

Leah snorted a laugh, releasing a long strand from the ball. "What do dead dreams smell like?" she asked.

"A frat house, mostly, but also like stale cheese balls." Jasmine stretched her legs out in front of her until her feet were resting against Leah's shins. "I was never big on the whole Santa thing. Who wants to think about a strange man breaking into your house once a year? It sounds like one of those ten creepiest moments videos you see on the internet."

"Sure," Leah agreed, nodding along. She leaned into the pressure against her shins, enjoying the proximity despite knowing that in a few days, it would all have meant nothing. The charade they were trying to pull off would be no more than a casual, occasional break room laugh between shifts. She tried not to think about it, but the inevitability of separation and of reality hung over her like an ominous cloud during tornado season. Whatever was going to happen, she could feel that it was going to be destructive. It would tear the roof from everything she'd spent years pushing down, and it would drown her in the flash flood of feelings.

Jasmine glanced at the television, black and silent. "Should we put a movie on?" she asked, already crawling across the floor to examine the cases stacked up on the shelf. "How about this one?" she suggested, pulling it free.

"No, Jazz, I hate that one," Annie protested. "It's depressing."

"It's a classic!" Jasmine argued, clutching the case to her chest. "It's an examination of self!"

Annie unwrapped another ornament, this one a ceramic dog in a bow tie. "It's depressing," she repeated. "It bums me out."

"Okay, fine," Jasmine relented, pressing it back into the space it had emerged from. "What about this one? You definitely can't say it's depressing, it's a comedy."

"Is that the one where—" Annie started.

Jasmine was already popping the case and sliding in the movie. "Yup!" she answered, reaching for the remote. "A modern classic, even if the reviewers hated it."

"Your grandmother and I tried to skip Christmas once," Martin said, now relaxing into the soft cushions of the couch, his loafer-style slippers planted on the rug. "I think we made it as far as December thirteenth before she caved. That woman could not resist a bake sale for a good cause, let me tell you." He adjusted the throw pillow, positioning it behind his head. "She raised almost five hundred dollars for underprivileged kids that year," he bragged. "More than twice what anyone else did. Her cupcakes were picture perfect." He shifted his gaze towards the kitchen, grinning mischievously. "Annie, where did those nice cakes go that Leah bought last night?"

"They went somewhere you wouldn't find them, old man," Annie shot back. "I know you, and you'd have devoured the entire box if left unattended."

Martin raised his hands wide, an innocent expression plastered across his face. "No one can say I'm unattended now, Annie. In fact, it's the most attended I've been all day." He jumped up off the couch, surprisingly spry for a man his age. "Come on, Annie, live a little." He did a little two-step on the rug, dancing towards the kitchen. "I'll make the hot chocolates if you free those cupcakes from their refrigerated prison."

"They aren't in the fridge or the freezer, but nice try," Annie said, climbing to her feet. "I was going to bring them out in a bit, but I guess now is as good a time as ever." She bent over the tangled lights, poking at one of the bulbs. "Do you girls want anything?"

Jasmine flashed Leah an encouraging look, her eyebrows raised in question.

"Uh, I'm a little peckish?" Leah asked, despite it being a statement. "Fast metabolism, you know."

Annie nodded, beckoning for her to follow. "Come on, let's raid the fridge," she said. "Dinner was pretty sparse at that hot dog stand on the way home, wasn't it? I might be a little hungry, too." She shuffled into the kitchen, pulling her long belted cardigan tight around her waist. "Dad, we're going to—how the heck did you find those?"

"You forget, I lived here first. I know all the good hiding spots." He set the box on the island like it was a trophy before digging through a wire basket of chocolate and marshmallows. "What are you foraging for?"

"That leftover chicken," Annie said, disappearing into the fridge. "It has to get eaten anyway." She dropped half a roasted chicken onto the counter, along with a tureen of loaded baked potato soup, half a loaf of sourdough bread, and a large bowl of mixed vegetables. "What do you think, Leah?" she asked. "Does this look okay?"

"Looks like a feast to me," Leah said, trying not to sound either too hungry or too casual. Midwestern hospitality required a careful balancing act of gratefulness that she hadn't quite mastered, even after living there for ten years. "Thank you."

They all sat around the coffee table in the living room, taking turns picking bits from the different plates, trading off the tangled lights back and forth until they were neatly looped around Jasmine's forearm, the plug clasped in her hands.

"Want to help me?" she asked, looking over at Leah. "I'm not quite tall enough to get it over the top by myself."

Leah stood before she was even done asking. "No problem," she answered, part of her eager to prove she was a good girlfriend, even when she was only temporary, and only around for two more days. Maybe it would be good enough for Jasmine to get a little breathing room. It was clear that her mother loved her, but she was a little intense.

"Hand me the other end," Leah said, ready to string the perfect tree. They wove the lights back and forth, their fingertips brushing each time until the strand was finished near the tip of the highest branch.

"I think you missed a spot," Annie whispered, not wanting to wake up her father, who was snoring softly on the sofa. "In the middle there, to the left."

Jasmine adjusted the lights until they were symmetrical, and she started to hang ornaments on the tree, filling gaps as she went, occasionally standing back to admire her work. Each ornament was logged in a notebook with the date, the cover scuffed and bent at the edges, and the paper inside curled from the basement's humidity.

"Are you always so meticulous?" Leah asked, watching her.

"I'm surprised you haven't noticed," Annie interjected. "She's always been like this. Everything has to be rank and file, placed in exactly the location it was before. Even her closet is organized not just by season, but by genre and color."

"I noticed that part," Leah said. "I suppose it beats my method of leaving clean laundry in the basket until it gets worn again. She handed Jasmine another ornament, this one a blown glass ball, swirled with peppermint stripes of green and red.

Annie picked through the box, unwrapping more ornaments, handing some to Jasmine, and placing others back in their slots. "I'll bet that drives you up the wall, Jazzy, doesn't it?" she asked, crumpling up some discarded paper towel. "You can't even bear to look at my closet."

"Oh, I, uh..." Jasmine started. She had no idea where Leah lived or with whom.

"I have roommates," Leah explained. It wasn't even a lie, and she was grateful for the crumb of truth. "Found them off a website. I don't really know either of them, we try to stay out of each other's hair. I wouldn't want to bring someone over, it's not that kind of place."

Annie cast a skeptical eye at Jasmine, and then at Leah. "You've never seen her place, Jazz?"

Jasmine shrugged, focusing on another ornament that didn't want to hang straight on the tree. "I have once or twice, we just don't hang out there. It's pretty small."

"It's not that small," Leah said, suddenly defensive even though she and Jasmine were supposedly on the same side. "I just never know when someone is going to be home or not, and I don't want to be the person always hogging the communal spaces." She took a string of tinsel garland from Annie, a thick, glittering snake of silver, and guided it around the tree, being careful to avoid hiding any of the ornaments. "But I'm hoping to move soon, so maybe I'll find someplace nicer."

"You're moving?" Jasmine blurted out. "When?"

"I don't know, not until my lease is up in the spring," Leah answered. "I hadn't mentioned it because I haven't given it much thought yet."

Jasmine's arms fell to her sides. "But you're staying in Rockland Heights, right?"

"I don't know, probably," Leah mumbled, suddenly feeling like she was being interrogated. "I figured we'd discuss it together." She'd hoped that would assuage the issue, but by the look on both their faces, she'd only inflamed it.

"I think three months is a little soon to be moving in together," Annie said, now standing with her hands on her hips. "I just don't want to see either of you hurt or in trouble."

"We're not moving in together," Jasmine interrupted, snatching the last ornament from the box. "Relax."

Leah snapped the lids back onto the empty boxes, stacking them in the corner. "We aren't?" she asked quietly, not sure if she was still supposed to be playing her role or not.

"Of course not," Jasmine said, snorting a laugh. "I could never leave Mom and Paps on their own, neither of them are at all organized."

Annie clipped her long braid to the top of her head, yawning. "I'm going to have to leave you two to it," she said. "I'm just about tapped out for the day."

"I'm not surprised, given how early you were up," Jasmine said. She snaked an arm around Leah's waist, pulling her closer. "I think we'll watch some movies before we turn in."

Chapter Twelve

Jasmine snuggled into Leah, both of them sharing the overstuffed chair in the soft glow of the tree's lights. "Let's watch yours first," she said, selecting movies from a menu on the television. "What's your pick?"

"We can wait for horror," Leah said, nodding towards Jasmine's grandpa. "I wouldn't want him to wake up to a man in a yeti costume, terrorizing skiers on the slopes in the Alps."

Jasmine laughed quietly, burying it in Leah's shoulder. "When you sell it like that, how am I supposed to resist the siren song of bad b-horror movies?" She readjusted her legs to hang over the side, the same way she had as a child. "He'll be alright, I promise. He willingly watches some of the worst movies I've ever seen. Most of them are from the seventies."

"Nostalgia comes for us all, I guess," Leah said, holding Jasmine in place with her lean, muscular arm. "But it's the twenty-third, we should at least pretend we're being festive, right?"

"Are you telling me that you want to watch a musical?" Jasmine asked, giving her a sideways glance. "Are you going to allow me to unleash my tyrannical power over the television with no repercussions or guidelines?" She looked over at her grandfather, still sleeping on the couch, his head tilted back and resting against the wall. "I know it wasn't part of the deal to watch movies with me."

"I'm a reasonable woman," Leah said, a smile tugging at the edges of her lips. "I'm more than willing to adjust the deal on the fly. I'm flexible."

Jasmine raised an eyebrow. "Yeah, I'll bet you are," she said, poking Leah in the bicep. "Wouldn't surprise me in the slightest."

"Okay, so what's this musical you want me to watch?" Leah asked, playfully trying to steal the remote. "Is it one of the old, super corny ones? The kind with so much schmaltz, I'm going to die of a sugar overdose?"

Jasmine wiggled herself closer, pressing Leah back into the seat despite her grandfather's quiet snores. She told herself her proximity to Leah was because he could wake up at any moment, and nothing more. "Is there any other kind?" she asked quietly. "If a musical doesn't rip out your heart and then clumsily glue it back together with an all-cast dance number, did you really see one?" She rested her hands on Leah's shoulders, pleasantly surprised at the strength there, hiding beneath green plaid and a black t-shirt. "How many musicals have you seen?"

"Maybe one or two in school," Leah replied. "I vividly remember being wildly underwhelmed." She took the remote from Jasmine's hands, craning her neck to scroll through the streaming service, looking for something, or maybe just playing around. "What could you possibly have that would be different?"

"Oh, I don't know, I bet we can find something decidedly whelming," Jasmine offered, taking the remote back, sliding the smooth black plastic out of Leah's lightly callused hands.

"Whelming," Leah replied, shaking her head. "What a rousing endorsement."

"Baby steps," Jasmine reassured her, twisting in the chair to find the musical she was looking for, one so over-the-top in its festive cheer, Leah might vomit glitter and candy canes onto the floor. "For haters, we start small."

Leah's mouth hung open, her face painted with mock indignation. "I'm not a *hater*," she defended, laughing quietly. "What is this, the nineties?"

"Pipe down, Erickson, I said what I said." Jasmine typed in the title one letter at a time, a frustrating experience with only a remote as guidance. "And yes, if you're wondering, I do fully anticipate retribution when you finally get hold of the television. I'm sure that, after this, you will choose the worst film ever made. You've probably already got one in mind, about evil mutant robots at a shopping mall."

Leah sucked her teeth, rolling her eyes. "Damn, you must have already seen that one."

"That's not real," Jasmine said, poking her in the ribs. "I was making it up."

"And yet, it exists," Leah insisted. "I have it on DVD and VHS." She shifted in the chair beneath Jasmine, settling her closer into her lap. "But yes, if you insist, I will sneak it into your locker at work, and you'll be so astounded that I wasn't lying, you will go home and watch it immediately, and then you'll be desperate for the next shift we work together so you can tell me what a work of genius it is."

Jasmine narrowed her eyes, having stopped on the movie she wanted them to watch together. "I don't believe you." She shrugged innocently, holding the remote out of Leah's reach. "I think you're lying to me."

"I'm not lying!" Leah said, laughing. "Give me your phone, I'll show you."

"Maybe I'd rather be surprised," Jasmine offered.

"You said you hate surprises," Leah countered, reaching for her phone. "And far be it from me to surprise you with anything other than a fantastic, god-tier, b-horror movie."

Jasmine intercepted Leah's hand, bringing it back to the chair as she interlaced their fingers. "I don't like surprises about anything big," she clarified. "No secret families, or hoards of wealth, or you know, arrests for murders, or anything."

Leah chuckled, shaking her head. "You should probably lay off the true crime podcasts, Reed. They're rotting your brain."

"Is this your confirmation that you don't have any prior arrests for murders?" Jasmine asked, reaching for a notebook. "Can I get that in writing?"

"I plead the fifth," Leah said, pushing the notebook out of her reach. "My secrets aren't anything special."

"Why have secrets at all?" Jasmine asked, surprised at the huskiness in her own voice. Leah stared back at her, hazel eyes dark but reflecting the bright white of the screen. She drew in a shaky breath and chewed on her lip, like maybe she was hiding something big. Maybe it was the same thing Jasmine had been ignoring for days.

"It's okay," Jasmine encouraged, pressing closer, with enough proximity that she could almost hear Leah's heart beating, pulsing at the artery in her neck. "I know how you feel."

"You do?" Leah asked, half-breathless.

Jasmine toyed with a lock of Leah's hair, twisting it around her finger before releasing it, letting it fall back to the side, draping over her ear. "I do." She leaned in, their lips almost brushing, when Leah spoke.

"Jasmine..." Leah trailed off, tightening her grip.

"What?" Jasmine asked, maintaining her proximity. "What's the matter? You're not preparing to leave early, are you?"

"No, it's just..." Leah shook her head. "Nothing. It's nothing."

Jasmine set the remote on the arm of the chair, relinquishing her power willingly. Whatever she'd thought the secret was, she'd been wrong, and she backed off from Leah, the sting of rejection burning as it sizzled across her face. "Was today too much? We can dial it back a little, we can go upstairs if you want, just go to bed, and tomorrow you can sleep in, if you want. Less contact, you know."

"Today wasn't too much," Leah answered. "It's not about that."

"Then what is it about?" Jasmine unfolded herself from the chair, stretching her arms over her head as she stood. "Listen, I know this was kind of a hare-brained idea in the first place, and truth be told, I didn't even think you'd go along with it. I suggested it as more of a joke."

"This is a joke to you?" Leah asked with too much quiet and calm to be that serene. She was too restrained, like a dam before bursting wide and flooding an entire city. "I thought you were serious about wanting me to do this."

"I was—I am!" Jasmine protested, her voice pressed down into a noisy whisper. "Leah, I should have been honest with you from the start, but I wanted them to relax because I applied for a new job downstate." She pulled at her fingers, an old nervous habit that had never quite left her. "I probably won't even get an interview, but I... I don't want to be at Syndicorp forever."

Leah stared at her and then shook her head. "And you think I do?" she retorted, acid eating at the edges of her words. "Do you think I wake up thrilled to work a split shift for a company that keeps me just barely below full-time so that I can't get healthcare?"

"No, of course not, I—" Jasmine started, losing track of her thoughts midway through her sentence.

"I have three roommates," Leah continued. "My car is fifteen years old, and between you and me, I'm not sure it's going to pass emissions testing this year." She ruffled her hair with frustration, pushing the longer bits back behind her ears, those silver rings glinting in the light from the tree. "I'm not happy with my lot in life, Jasmine, I'm just finding it incredibly difficult to make anything else happen for the better."

Jasmine reached out for Leah's arm, but retreated when Leah flinched away from her touch. "I know," she said softly. "We're not so different. My roommates are just them, you know, but it's different. They... can be overbearing."

"I asked you to cover those shifts for me because despite being broke as hell ten minutes after I get paid, I can't be at work those days. I agreed to pretend to be your girlfriend because that was the deal on the table, and I couldn't afford not to take it." Leah drew her knees up to her chest, crushing herself back into the wingback chair, the dark plaid fabric almost black in the dim light.

"Why can't you work those shifts?" Jasmine asked.

"I told you already," Leah shot back. "Some of us have difficult cycles."

Jasmine leaned in closer, bracing her palms against the arm of the chair. "I don't believe you. I don't think that's why, or you'd be asking for shift swaps every damned month. I might be new, but I'm able to check a swaps clipboard and see that you rarely ask people to cover shifts for you."

"What are you, a private eye or something?" Leah snapped. "No, I don't, because usually I just request the days off, and when it's not within three days of a major holiday that's centered around gifts and excess, it's not a problem." She hugged her knees tightly, turning her face towards the wall. "If you were so suspicious of me, why invite me here?"

"I... don't know," Jasmine answered truthfully.

Leah exhaled a sardonic laugh through her nose. "Great," she muttered.

"I told you, I don't like big surprises," Jasmine reiterated. "And I thought maybe you'd tell me the truth if we hung out a little bit. I thought maybe you'd start to trust me enough." She tugged at the string of her hoodie, pulling it as far as it would go. "I guess not."

"It's been two days," Leah replied acerbically. "Some things require a little more investment than that. I told you the truth of it, but clearly, that's not enough."

Jasmine folded her arms over her chest, backing up until she was in the doorway. "Yeah, clearly," she echoed softly, looking sideways at her grandpa, who let out a quiet snore. At least they hadn't woken him up—they were being reckless by discussing it at all. "I think I should go to bed."

"Yeah, maybe you should," Leah agreed, turning to face the screen. "I'll see you in the morning."

Chapter Thirteen

A tear gathered in the corner of Leah's eye, but she wasn't sure whether it was exhaustion, the upcoming moon, the movie, or the awful conversation with Jasmine. She brushed it away, trying to ignore her feelings on the subject.

The film played quietly on the television, the scenes flashing colors against the wall, mixing and muddying with the glow of the lights from the tree. It had only been a few hours between something that felt like cautious hope, and something that felt like an all-too-familiar sense of abject failure. If nothing else, at least she was used to the sensation.

"This is one of Jazzy's favorites, you know," Martin said, peering at the screen through one open eye. "Where is she, anyway?"

"Upstairs," Leah answered. "She was tired. I decided to watch the movie on my own. Couldn't sleep, you know?"

He nodded thoughtfully, yawning and stretching his arms over his head. "I'm such an old man now, falling asleep on the sofa." He checked his wristwatch, shifting to the edge of the cushion with excitement. "My tumbler!" he exclaimed softly. "Sorry, please forgive an old man his boring hobbies." He stood, but hesitated in the doorway. "Are you staying up?"

Leah shrugged. "I guess. Might as well finish the movie."

"Are you partial to midnight snacks?" He squinted at his watch again. "Though I suppose we're past that now, it's closer to one in the morning."

"I'm probably okay," she lied, already planning how she'd silently unwrap a granola bar upstairs, one careful movement at a time. "But you go ahead."

Martin disappeared into the kitchen, almost silent except for the telltale crinkle of a bag of chips, and, if she had to guess, the tab of a can of soda, followed by the creak of the garage door hinge.

The musical was almost saccharine, yet it was slowly pulling her apart, one ensemble number at a time. Two people, pretending to be engaged for the benefit of others. If Leah had watched it even two weeks prior, she would have rolled her eyes and resented the time she'd wasted. But in the midst of her own dubiously moral undertaking, it was starting to test the load-bearing support beams she'd long had in place to keep the flood of her emotions in check. The brackets were cracked, and she was already doomed.

"Okay," Martin said, re-entering the living room with an armful of odd assortments. He dumped two family-sized bags of chips on the table, different kinds, along with a four-pack of mini dips, some cans of soda linked together with a blue cardboard label, and curiously, a rock tumbler.

Leah sat up straight in the chair, pausing the film, grateful for the distraction. "Jasmine didn't mention you liked to tumble rocks," she said.

"What's it to you?" Martin asked, arranging the snacks on the coffee table. "Are you an interested party?"

"I'm a geologist," Leah replied. "Well, kind of. I have a graduate degree, but I work with Jasmine at Syndicorp."

"A geologist!" he almost shouted, and then looked at the stairs warily, worried he'd woken up the others. "I'm certainly not as skilled as you, no, certainly not, but I guess you could call me a hobbyist." He held the black container under his arm, looking over at Leah. "Do you want to rinse them out with me? This is the final pass, fine grit media."

"I thought you'd never ask." Leah trailed after him into the kitchen, hitting the light switch as she went. "So what have you got in here this time?"

"I'm not sure, it was a mystery pack, and I'm not amazing at identifying everything before it's tumbled." Martin opened the hatch, dumping a slurry of mineral-laden water and coated bits of rock into a colander. "Don't tell Annie, she hates when I do this in here, but it's cold as heck outside and I'm reasonably certain the garden hose is frozen."

Leah laughed, leaning against the counter with one hand. "Your secret is safe with me."

He doused the colander with cold water, revealing the shining, smooth rocks. Martin's face lit up with every rock that became visible, glistening with water under the incandescent bulbs overhead. "This is a good batch," he whispered, poking at one of the larger rocks. "Look! Tigerseye!"

"That's a nice one," Leah agreed, taking it when he offered it. "Nice striations. A wonderful example of a metamorphic rock, even if it's leaning into the quartz category."

"Is it really?" Martin asked, taking it back from her to hold it to the light. "And what sort of rock is your favorite?"

"Oh, plenty, but one takes first prize," Leah replied, taking over the rinsing. "Ruby Zoisite, red corundum mixed in with green zoisite. It's unique and beautiful, and a stunning example of two things being better when together than apart." Water flooded the rocks, taking the mud and silt with it as it exited the holes of the strainer. "It's always so fascinating to look at a rock and see all the history there that predates us by thousands of years."

Martin began to pluck the rocks out one at a time, drying them with a soft cloth. "I think that's part of the appeal, isn't it, with rocks?"

Leah tilted her head, turning off the tap. "What do you mean?"

"I mean, sure, rocks are subject to entropy, but the scale of time is so immense, we can't even begin to wrap our human brains around the enormity of it." He shined one of the rocks up, setting it on the island. "People are so concerned about legacy, when our time here on Earth is such an absurd little blip. Why we've chosen, as a species, to fill that time with red tape and paperwork, is beyond me."

"I'm not sure what I think about legacy," Leah answered, once again taken aback at how easily the truth was spilling from her lips. "As for the enormity of time, it's..." she trailed off, searching for the right word. "Oppressive."

Martin nodded thoughtfully, continuing to work through the small pile of rocks. "It's too much time," he said. "We can't comprehend it."

"To our detriment," Leah said. "We are creatures who are fundamentally impatient. If something doesn't impact us right now, or even in our lifetimes, we have no need for it. We discard it, along with all the rest of the warnings from the past." She picked out another stone, this one a beautiful teal blue.

"Turquoise!" Martin exclaimed, taking it lovingly into his hands.

Leah shook her head. "It's howlite," she corrected. "Softer." She leaned over, pressing her short fingernail into the surface. "See?"

"And those pieces at the festive fair?" he asked, pulling a pair of reading glasses from his pocket. "The ones near the entrance? Turquoise or howlite?"

"Probably turquoise," Leah answered. "Lots of bracelets, if it was howlite they'd all wind up damaged."

He nodded silently, taking everything in, and Leah had forgotten how much fun it was digging through rocks. She was resisting the impulse to start word-vomiting back half the textbooks she'd read in college. Martin set down the stone, returning to the others. "You know, my Marsha loved opalite," he said softly. "Called them moonstones, didn't even care they weren't really from the moon. I told her time and time again that they were man-made, no one dug it out of the earth. Do you know what she told me?"

Leah shook her head.

"Marsha told me that she loved it because it showed the ingenuity of humans alongside the love of all things beautiful, and that those two things combined were what makes us real." He plucked another rock out, rubbing the cloth against it. "That's stayed with me longer than most things, I suspect."

"Is that why you got into rock tumbling?" Leah asked.

"In part," he replied. "It was a gift from Annie about five years back. I don't think she thought I would take to it like a duck to water." He nudged in next to Leah, rinsing out the casing. "Annie... she means well, you know."

"Of course she does, she's Jasmine's mother," Leah replied, feigning ignorance about Annie's overbearing, overprotective nature.

Martin sighed heavily, setting the container into the drying rack, where water ran out in rivulets, then slowed to a trickle. "It was hard for her when Jazzy was sick," he explained. "Always in and out of the hospital, you know, I'm sure Jasmine has told you."

Leah didn't want to lie, so instead of replying, or nodding her head, she just made a quiet murmur of encouragement.

"Jasmine's brother needed a kidney. The guy was suffering for so long, no donors, no hope of finding one in time. He was always on dialysis up in the city, and Jasmine started taking the train up to visit him when he was there. After a while, she started making noise about getting tested to see if she was a match." Martin collected the shining rocks, sweeping them into his palm where they rattled, almost too loud for that time of night. "Annie was dead against it from the start, but Jasmine was eighteen, so what could she do?"

"It can't have been easy," Leah offered, hitting the light switch on her way out of the kitchen. Her stomach rumbled angrily, and Martin laughed.

"Sounds like maybe you should join me for that snack," he suggested, waving a hand at the coffee table. "Take a seat. No reservations needed."

Leah sat opposite the couch on the floor, her legs folded beneath her like a pretzel. "Thanks," she said, plucking a ridged chip from one of the bags and dipping it into a sauce. "I love these."

"Anyway, Jasmine and Damien share a dad, you know." Martin frowned, his forehead creased in anger, an unusual expression for him, at least it had been for the past two days. He cleared his throat quietly, reaching for a soda and popping the top, taking a loud slurp from the top. "He's..." Martin trailed off, shaking his head. "I shouldn't be uncharitable this time of year, but let's just say he's not particularly reliable. Never once went to see Damien, never offered to get tested. Never visited Jazz on any of her many stays, either."

"I can't imagine that," Leah said between bites. "I think the guilt would eat me alive."

"Some people don't feel it," Martin said. "They're the ones to watch out for if you ask me." He dragged a handful of chips out of the bag, eating them out of his hand instead. "And Annie took the brunt of it. The never-ending doctor visits, blood work, and medical bills. She didn't want to move back here, but I insisted."

"That was nice of you," Leah offered, taking a can of soda for herself. The green aluminum had a strange hue in the glow of the living room, but the sugary taste was enough to slow the shakes in her hands from not eating enough.

"Nah, it was more for me than for them," Martin said. "I was rattling around in this place all on my own. I didn't want to live here by myself, not so soon after Marsha—well, you know." He shook more chips out of the bag, the salty crumbs coating the glass of the table. "I practically begged Annie to give up that old drafty place twenty miles up the road, spent months convincing her it was no imposition to move back into her childhood home. Here was closer to the hospital, Jasmine's doctors..." He shrugged again, heaving out a heavy sigh. "And I wasn't sure how more much longer I could bear the loneliness."

"It's too much," Leah agreed, being all too familiar with the sensation of isolation.

Martin gave her a strange look that she couldn't quite decipher, but the intensity unsettled her. "If you find something special, Leah, you have to hold onto it. Don't let it fade into the background. Seize it." He smiled, crunching on another chip. "What's the saying? Seize the carp?"

"Carpe diem," Leah answered, almost choking on the laugh that had lodged a piece of a chip in her throat. She swigged from the can, willing it to dislodge, painfully aware that the longer it went on, the redder her face would get.

"Yeah, that," Martin said, his face both bemused and concerned. "Are you alright?"

"I'm fine," Leah coughed, drinking more green sugary soda from the can until her throat was assuaged. "I'm fine," she repeated, hoping it was more convincing. "I don't enjoy the feeling of being alone," she said finally. "It's like being slowly pressed into olive oil."

"Well, at least you haven't had that feeling for a few months, right?" he asked, averting his eyes just long enough that Leah wondered how much he'd heard earlier that night.

"A little longer," Leah lied. "We were friends first, you know, from work."

Martin funneled the last of the open bag into his mouth, catching most of the crumbs, but not all of them. "I knew Marsha was the one the moment I laid eyes on her. She was dancing in a mud puddle with half-dead flowers in her hair, laughing so loud she was snorting." He shifted in his seat, hands pressed down into the worn upholstery, the green velvet long since threadbare in some places. "I'd seen her around, you know, a friend of a friend, but never like that. I vowed in that moment that I'd get up the guts to ask her out."

"It obviously worked," Leah said, reaching for the other bag.

"Oh, yeah," Martin said, draining his can of soda. "We were going steady by the end of the weekend. When you know, you know."

"The first time I saw Jasmine, I was wondering what the heck she was doing in Rockland Heights," Leah admitted. "Her hair was tied back into a ponytail with one of those clip things." She mimed the shape of it with her hands, trying to show how it worked. "It doesn't matter what her hair was doing," she said. "I just... wanted her to talk to me." Leah dipped another chip into the creamy dip, letting the acidity of the onions gently sizzle on her tongue before she swallowed. Wanting Jasmine to talk to her, at least, wasn't a lie. That much was true.

"This is the longest Annie and Jasmine have gone without having a huge argument in years," he said casually. "Usually, they're at each other's throats almost every day. Jasmine wants freedom, Annie wants her to be safe." He stole a chip from Leah's pile with a mischievous grin. "Unstoppable force and an immovable object." He smacked his hands against his knees, groaning as he stood up. "I'll have to leave you with the rest, I'm afraid I'm turning into a pumpkin."

Leah took his seat on the sofa, poised with the remote to watch the rest of the movie. "Pumpkins aren't in season, Martin."

Chapter Fourteen

Jasmine had been lying awake since five in the morning, irritatingly aware that Leah wasn't there, but too scared to descend the stairs to find her, because she'd probably already left. Leah had probably gotten into her car and driven home, despite it being in the middle of the night, and still with two days to go in their deal.

Her alarm chirped, and she leaned over to smack the little orange box back to sleep. It was eight, and she was still exhausted, and now hungry, too. She could fight the curious urge to know where Leah had gone, but she couldn't fight the impulse to raid the kitchen, devouring everything half-decent she found in the fridge before her mother woke up and started to panic about not having enough for Christmas, even though it was just the four of them.

Dragging herself out of the sheets, she shuffled to the bathroom to perform the morning ritual of a shower, scrubbing suds into her hair, drenching it with a thick, viscous conditioner, and exfoliating her skin, thinking too much about how nice it had felt pressed up against Leah the night before.

"Get hold of yourself, Reed," she muttered at her reflection, pointing with the hairbrush. "This was only ever supposed to be the means to an end."

She shoved her pajamas into the wicker hamper, cramming down the overflowing liner with a balled fist. Laundry could be a problem *after* the holidays. Plugging in the hair dryer, she shivered on the cold tiles, wishing they had heated floors. Jasmine went through the motions, part of her still half-asleep, and the other part dreading having to address the previous evening's conversation, or discovering that Leah had fled.

She couldn't blame Leah if she had run, after all, they'd already smacked directly into several awkward conversations with her family, a near miss, and probably more discomfort than she had bargained for when she'd agreed to Jasmine's plan.

The heat from the hair dryer was hot and dry against her skin as she placed it beneath her shirt, desperate for warmth after losing so much to the damp room, cold seeping beneath the window. The temperature had dropped overnight from a usual December cold into a frigid icebox.

Jasmine crept out of the bathroom when she finished, leaving the door ajar so that the room would air out from the steam, and not just collect on the floor, pooling where the tiles were slightly uneven. Her mother's door was still closed, and so was her grandpa's. It was at least some relief, knowing they hadn't woken up during her shower and discovered for themselves that Leah had already left without a word. It would be difficult to explain, but with some coffee, a muffin, and a pile of scrambled eggs, she might just come up with a feasible answer.

One stair at a time, she slunk down the stairs in her slippers, rubbing her hands together for the warmth of friction.

"Good morning," Leah said, standing in the kitchen doorway with a steaming mug. "I made coffee."

"Oh," Jasmine said, taking the cup into her hands. "I thought you left."

Leah tilted her head quizzically. "Why would I leave?"

"We had an argument—or a disagreement, I don't know." Jasmine took a sip, the liquid heating her core, and she leaned in closer to it, clutching it to her chest, absorbing the heat even through her thick sweater. "How did you know I was about to come downstairs?"

"I heard the shower," Leah answered. "Figured it was probably you. Hoped it was you, I guess."

"I'm sorry I pried."

"Jasmine..." Leah trailed off, pouring herself a mug from the pot. "Listen, I'm not trying to be weird or cagey, it's just... hard." She cupped her hands around the mug, mirroring Jasmine. "I haven't really had anyone close for a while."

"I get it." Jasmine took a hesitant step forward, but stopped at the island, perching at the edge of a stool, unwilling to set down the mug. "You just kind of get used to keeping it all inside."

Leah nodded, but still wouldn't make eye contact. "I promise it's not illegal."

"That's a good start," Jasmine replied, stifling a giggle. "I wouldn't have suspected you of that, you have too much golden retriever energy."

"I have *what?*" Leah asked, almost incredulous.

"You know, loyal, good, friendly," Jasmine supplied. "Kind. And you have nice hair."

Leah's nose scrunched up in disgust. "I hate my hair this long."

"I like it." Jasmine shrugged easily, poking a pack of muffins, encased in plastic. "Want one?"

"No thanks," Leah answered. "I don't think we're done with this golden retriever thing yet." She set her coffee on the counter, rolling up the sleeves of her plaid shirt until her forearms were exposed, hinting at hidden tattoos. "I'd like to open negotiations for what dog breed I am."

Jasmine snorted. "I don't think that's how it works," she said apologetically. "It's not like anyone is out here saying someone has, I don't know, greyhound energy. Or spaniel energy, or—"

"I think I'd be more of a bear," Leah announced.

"You don't get to pick your own familiar," Jasmine protested. "Someone has to assign it to you. And we were talking about dogs, not large and terrifying predators."

Leah looked at her now, an eyebrow raised in challenge. "Fine, then I'd be a mixed breed, the kind where no one can really tell what they are."

"Why?"

"No one ever wants those in the shelters, but they're the most loyal." Leah took a muffin, peeling off the paper wrapper. "What kind is this?"

"Banana nut," Jasmine answered. "Hold up there, partner, we're not done examining this yet. You feel like an unwanted shelter dog?"

Leah took a large bite of the muffin, catching the crumbs in her outstretched hand below. "Not in a sad way, in a *once I find the right home I'll be loyal to the end of my days* sort of way."

"And you haven't yet?" Jasmine freed her own muffin from the paper, but kept the crumbs more contained, not wanting to dirty the island so early in the morning. There would be time enough for that once her mother woke up.

"Thought I did once or twice, got returned to the shelter. Metaphorically." Leah sneaked a glance at her, only for a second. "If I can't be a bear, then I'm a mixed breed shelter dog." Leah was already finished, and flexed her arm, much to Jasmine's delight and surprise. "Bears are pretty strong, you know."

"So I've heard," Jasmine said. "But I wouldn't mind you proving that later." She nodded towards Leah's flex, but despite her attempt at being suave, her face heated from the neck up, the redness of her blush visible even in the distorted reflection of the microwave door. "Sorry, I just—"

"Bear or shelter dog," Leah reiterated. "Say it."

"What is your problem with golden retrievers?" Jasmine demanded playfully, grateful for the redirection. "Did one bite you as a kid or something?"

"No, they just aren't me." Leah picked up the coffee pot, poised over her mug. "Say it, or I drink the rest right now."

"Playing hardball?" Jasmine asked. "There are more coffee beans in the cabinet. Your threat is empty, Erickson."

Leah poured a splash of coffee and stopped. "Yeah, but this pot takes at least fifteen minutes to brew. Can your coffee-loving self wait that long?" She dolloped another swallow's worth into her cup, staring in challenge.

Jasmine considered her options, enjoying the banter too much, and not wanting it to end. They were playing parts, just in case anyone walked in, but there was the tiniest sparkle of genuine affection, and it was tugging on her fragile heart strings. "You've called my bluff," she said finally, nudging her half-empty mug across the island. "You have bear energy, Leah Erickson."

"Thank you," Leah said, nodding. "The universe has righted itself." She topped off the mug, emptying the pot in the process. "I'll make more," she offered, and started the process, not even waiting for a reply. "I always thought maybe I'd get a dog someday, when I don't have a million different roommates." She peered out the frosty window, frowning at the wintery landscape. "*If* that ever happens."

"It will," Jasmine reassured her, all too conscious of their argument the night before. "You'll get the sad-but-loyal shelter dog of your dreams, I just know it."

"Morning!" her mother chirped, all decked out in her Christmas Eve finery of a tinsel-laden sweater, festive print leggings, reindeer slippers, and a headband striped like a candy cane. "I am positively shocked to see both of you up before me. Usually the kiddos only do that on Christmas day." She winked, taking her polar bear mug out of the cabinet. "And coffee, too," she exclaimed, taking the pot. "Leah is a keeper, Jazzy, you'd better not let this one go."

"Uh, yeah," Jasmine said, flashing an apologetic glance at Leah. "She makes good coffee. And sorry, we broke into the muffins already."

Her mother sat at the kitchen table with her coffee, inhaling the steam. "It's fine, there are emergency muffins hidden in the bottom drawer." She opened one eye, looking over at Jasmine. "Don't tell Paps."

"I would never," Jasmine replied, drawing an x over her chest in promise. "Cross my heart. Unless he bribes me with something good." She finished her breakfast, tossing the paper into the garbage can. "Leah, you were up last night with him, what did you two get up to?"

"Er..." Leah trailed off, turning away. "We did have a small snack. Sorry if it was corralled for the holidays."

"Nonsense!" Jasmine's mother chastised. "You are our guest. My father is a feral thing who ferrets out all the best stuff." She waved at the counter, stocked with snacks and baking supplies. "Please, Leah, help yourself."

"I'm fine for now, thank you," Leah replied.

"So!" Jasmine interrupted, attempting to slice through the strange tension with sharp, unrelenting cheeriness. "It's Christmas Eve. What are we doing today? The tree is up, most of the food is prepared—Mom, do you need help with anything? Turkey, sides? Peeling potatoes?"

"Paps is doing all that," her mother said, still hovering over her coffee. "Far be it from me to tell him no." She wrapped her hands around the mug, the stone rings on her thumb clinking delicately against the ceramic. "You could hit up some last minute shopping, both of you, if you wanted."

Despite the mall being the last place she wanted to be that day, Jasmine turned to Leah with a hopeful smile. "What do you think? It's not far from here. I could drive if you want, my car is smaller. Easier to find a parking space."

"Uh, sure," Leah replied, rinsing her mug in the sink. "I'm game for whatever. Usually I'm working today, but they gave it to Greg. I wish they'd given it to me and let me have the twenty-sixth, at least."

"You work the day after Christmas?" Jasmine's mother asked, her tone colored by her horror. "How awful."

Leah shrugged. "I don't usually mind. It's better than the first week in January, that's really when things start to get intense."

"So you'll be leaving us when? Tomorrow night? The morning after?" Jasmine's mother pressed, too curious for her own good, as far as Jasmine was concerned, especially since Jasmine had agreed to take that shift. "You could come back that night, if you don't mind the drive."

"Mom, lay off," Jasmine warned. "You know how tiring those shifts are. Leah will come back, just not immediately after a nine-hour shift dealing with people who don't know how to put things back on a shelf after they decided they don't want something."

"I'm sorry, Mrs—er—Annie," Leah stammered. "I tried to get the days off, but they scheduled me anyway. That's why Jas—"

"Anyway," Jasmine interrupted, shooting Leah a look, "we should get going. The mall is only open until four, and it's going to get wilder and hairier the longer we leave it."

Her mother's stare flicked from Jasmine's face to Leah's, and back again, suspicion etched into every fine line. "Pick me up some of those candles, if you get a chance?" she asked. "We're all out, and those other ones have a weird smell."

"Blackberry sunrise, got it," Jasmine confirmed. "Leah, do you want to change? Or—uh—maybe I'll just go change, actually."

Leah hovered in the doorway, leaning against the frame with her forearm. "I should change," she confirmed, allowing Jasmine to wriggle out of the awkward moment. "I can't have the fine folks at the shopping mall think I wore the same outfit two days in a row." She gave Jasmine an apologetic nod and disappeared up the stairs, each step creaking noisily as she went.

"Don't be out too late," her mother warned. "You know how people get on the roads this time of year. Too much alcohol, not enough sense." She finally took a sip of her coffee, letting the taste settle in her mouth before she swallowed. "I didn't hear either of them go to bed last night, did you?" she asked.

"It was late," Jasmine answered, hoping she could continue to obfuscate the truth until the end of Christmas. Two more days, that was it. "I think it was around three or so."

"Three!" her mother exclaimed. "I'm starting to feel like the odd one out, having the only normal circadian rhythm in the house."

Jasmine laughed quietly, the muted sound exhaled through her nose with caution. "Leah works nights sometimes, I imagine that's why," she offered. She had no way of knowing if it was true or not, so she'd have to remind herself to warn Leah about that potential line of questioning she'd get later. "I don't know about Paps. Maybe he's just built that way."

Her mother tugged the previous day's newspaper closer to herself, unfolding the first page. "I don't even know why we have this delivered anymore, it's not like we have a need. It's all drivel now, anyway." She tore off a page, crumpling it in one hand and throwing it across the kitchen to land atop the garbage bag, just next to a bag of discarded vegetable ends. "Aren't you going to change, too? Or are you going in your pajamas?"

"I figured I would just wait until Leah's done," Jasmine replied. If there was anything her mother couldn't argue with, it was Midwestern hospitality ethics.

Her mother nodded thoughtfully, turning page after page until she reached the real estate section, which she tore out for herself. "You could change, too, you know," she said casually. "You're both grown adults."

Jasmine's hand froze on the kitchen door's handle. "Oh... okay."

"We've never been prudish about that, Jazzy." Her mother winked, and Jasmine cringed. As grateful as she was for their support, they didn't have to be so awkward about it.

The steps creaked under her movement, too. She coughed loudly on the stairs, hoping it would announce her presence in a more casual way, and hopefully in a way that didn't feel very strange to be a part of. "Leah?" she called softly through the door. "I just needed to grab something that isn't pajamas."

"Mmhmm," Leah mumbled from within.

Jasmine nudged open the door, confronted with the sight of a topless Leah. "Oh my God," she said, slamming the door again. "Sorry! I thought you said it was fine!"

"It's fine," Leah said, revealing herself again, this time clothed. She pulled Jasmine inside and closed them inside, a black tank top draped over her hand. She was lean, muscular like a swimmer, taut biceps and veins running along her forearms parallel to her tattoos, the long, undulating lines of a topographical map stretching from wrist to shoulder. "Shh," she urged. "You don't want them to hear all that."

"Right," Jasmine said, nodding. "I'm sorry anyway." She tried to avert her eyes, but struggled to tear her gaze away from the outline of Leah's abs, prominent against her pale, porcelain skin, the contrast stark next to her black sports bra. "I'm sorry," she repeated for the third time.

"I told you, it's fine," Leah said, pulling on the tank top and tucking it into her acid-washed jeans. "We all have bodies."

Jasmine busied herself inside the closet, a welcome respite after considering burning out her eyeballs to keep herself from staring. "That's a very calm take on the situation," she muttered, sliding hangers from left to right as she searched for something to wear.

"Would you rather I was upset about it?" Leah asked, sitting on the bed to pull on a fresh pair of thick socks. "Would yelling about that make things easier?"

"No," Jasmine admitted, selecting a thick sweater and a pair of black jeans. "Let's just go, the sooner we're out of their range, the better."

Chapter Fifteen

Shopping malls may as well have been the seventh circle of hell at any point in the year for Leah, but something about being there on Christmas Eve made the experience that much more intolerable. Jasmine swore under her breath repeatedly, each time someone stole a parking spot she was aiming for.

"We can just leave," Leah offered, praying that her suggestion would be taken.

Jasmine shook her head. "No, my mom asked me to get those candles because she knew I forgot to get them for her for Christmas. Paps and I promised her we'd get enough to last the year, and we both totally spaced." She jerked the car to the left, edging into a spot at the back of the lot. Another car honked at her, and she offered an apologetic wave. "Sorry!" she yelled. "Good luck out there!"

The car in park, Jasmine unbuckled her belt and pocketed the keys. "You can stay in the car if you want."

"Nah," Leah said. "I heard they have funnel cakes in there." She gave Jasmine what she thought was a convincing smile and pulled on the handle, releasing the door's latch. "Besides, what kind of fake girlfriend would I be if I abandoned you to the zombified hordes of Christmas shoppers?"

Jasmine clicked the key fob, staring off towards the mall's entrance. "I appreciate the backup. Last year it was me and Paps, and he is a terrible mission wingman. He gets distracted by everything shiny, he's like a crow."

"I'll do my best to stay on task," Leah replied, stifling a laugh because it was starting to worry her how easily she joked in Jasmine's presence. "But I will be demanding a visit to the food court as payment."

Their boots crunched and slid through murky sludge, the product of half-melted snow and ice settling into the crevices of their treads. Even from outside the shopping mall, it was obvious that it was heaving with people, all of them sardined into the shops and foyer, overtired kids screaming, their frenzied parents clutching coffees, their last attachment to keeping it together.

"Ready?" Jasmine asked, yanking on the entrance door.

"Commence mission," Leah replied, steeling herself against the crowds. It wouldn't be long, and they'd be back in the car, safe from the noise and the fervor of last-minute shoppers. "Operation: candles is a go."

"Left," Jasmine said, tugging on Leah's sleeve. "The Candlebath store is just around the corner."

Leah nodded, following her through the throngs of people, repeating "excuse me" every few seconds as people bumped into her. That close to a full moon, the urge to push people away from her was strong, but she had half a lifetime of quiet practice and retail work to lean on, at least for a little while longer. It would be harder once night fell. "Oh, no," she murmured, spotting the long line stretching from the store's entrance all the way to the back of the shopping mall.

"What the hell," Jasmine hissed. "It wasn't like this last year."

"There's my guess," Leah said, pointing at a sign indicating select products were half off. "We should have gotten here earlier. Sorry."

Jasmine slid into place at the back of the line, tugging off her mittens and shoving them into her pockets. "Maybe it will move fast," she offered, but there was a hopelessness in her voice that was palpable, even above the din of the mall. "I shouldn't have dragged you with me."

"Hey, it was me or your Paps," Leah said. "At least I won't get distracted." She unzipped her leather jacket, already too warm in the overheated building and feeling pins beneath her skin. She had to move, had to walk off the urge to shift early. "Is there anything else you need to get? I could run off and grab it while you wait."

"What's the matter, you don't like lines?" Jasmine asked, leaning against the brick wall.

"I'm impatient," Leah answered, again too truthful for her comfort. "I like to be moving from one thing to the next."

Jasmine raised one bemused eyebrow, tucking a stray lock of dark hair behind her ear. "Like a shark?"

Leah shrugged. "Sure, like a shark."

"You could go get us some snacks," Jasmine suggested. "I know it hasn't been long since breakfast, but muffins don't fill me up for long. There's a boba place in the food court, they might still have some of the taro if we're lucky."

"Taro?" Leah asked. "I've never had boba."

"It's a drink made from a starchy root vegetable, it's purple," Jasmine explained. "No, don't give me that face, Erickson, it's good, I promise." She shuffled forward an inch or two with the movement of the line, wiggling her eyebrows. "Better hurry, this line is zooming."

Leah made a note in her phone, knowing she'd never remember the order once she found the boba place, not when her thoughts were already scrambled from the heat and the crowds. "Anything else?"

"A winning lottery ticket," Jasmine instructed. "Don't worry, we'll split the proceeds fifty–fifty."

"Oh, okay, I'll just go pick one up then," Leah replied, deadpan despite the rising panic that was crawling across her lower back. "Might as well make it three winning lottery tickets, right? And a private jet?"

"Yeah, but make sure the seats are leather. I hate the cloth seats, too hard to clean." Jasmine's nose scrunched up as she giggled to herself, laughing at her own joke. "And don't forget the crate of expensive champagne either, we'll need celebration supplies."

"I didn't think you drank much," Leah said, forgetting that they were playing a game.

"I don't, but if I win the lottery, who cares about medical bills?" Jasmine said casually. "I'll just buy myself an extra kidney on the black market. Boom. Done."

"Merry Christmas, here's your new kidney?" Leah prompted, shifting her weight from hip to hip in anticipation of running the snack errand, desperate to get away from the growing line behind them. "Is that how it would go?"

Jasmine took off her hat, her hair staticky beneath. "Nah, mine is bigger now. I would just save the black market kidney money for a brand new top-of-the-line motorcycle."

"You're a biker?"

"No, but I bet you could be," Jasmine replied, tugging at the zipper of Leah's jacket. "You've already got half the outfit." She glanced at her phone, checking the time before shoving it into her back pocket. "You'd better hurry, or all they'll have left is the strawberry milk boba, which I hate and revile."

"Noted." Leah fumbled for the wallet in her inside jacket pocket, making sure it was still there. "I'll be back in a few."

***

Leah sidled her way through the flowing crowd, wondering why she seemed to be going in the opposite direction as everyone else. A man nearly bowled her over, crashing into her with his half dozen huge handled bags stuffed to the brim with tissue paper.

"Sorry," he called over his shoulder as he got carried away by the tide of the innumerable people.

The lights overhead were too bright, and she could swear they were emitting some sort of high-pitched screeching sound that no one else seemed to be able to hear. She wanted to pull her jacket over her head and crush herself into a corner, yet everyone else was noisily finishing their gift shopping.

She supposed that at the very least, she wasn't working at the store. The smallest of mercies, when surrounded by a horde of eager shoppers.

Her skin rippled uncomfortably, and she squeezed her eyes shut for a split second, trying to envision anywhere other than where she was. "No," she whispered aloud to herself, the sound getting lost amidst the cacophony of the mall. "Not here, not now." She took three deep breaths, holding them, and exhaling as she braced against the glass window of a sporting goods store. She was almost about to regain her composure when a child barreled into her legs, knocking her over.

Immediately afterward, after the kid had shrieked with surprise and been hoisted off the ground by their parent, a stroller smacked into Leah's back.

"Hey!" the teenager pushing it yelled, the seat filled with bags. "Watch where you're going!"

"Sorry," Leah mumbled, pulling herself to her feet again. The main atrium in the mall was wall-to-wall people, and she wasn't even sure how she was going to get to the other side in the first place to get Jasmine's tea, snacks, and some air. If she didn't get a breather soon, she'd wind up on the nightly news, an escaped bear in the Rockland Heights shopping mall. She'd get darted if she was lucky, and shot if she wasn't. Mall cops would love an excuse to scrape glory from her furry, oversized corpse.

She tried making her way through the crowd towards the escalator, getting pushed to the side by three other people before she'd even taken five steps. Each time it happened, she got closer to an early shift, almost feeling the fur poke up through the skin on her arms already. "No," she hissed, pushing past a group of young men in matching ski parkas. "No, no," she said again, getting knocked back by an elderly man wielding a surprisingly heavy cane.

Her spine crunched, the first sign that a shift into her Bear form was inevitable. Panic flooded through her veins, which only made matters worse. Adrenaline was a frequent cause of early or out-of-cycle shifts, and with the full moon only a day and a half away, her body was aching to let loose, to shift, to bellow at everyone and send them scattering, leaving her in blissful, uninterrupted peace.

Until emergency services arrived, of course. And that was assuming she'd be able to outrun the mall cops.

Leah crashed into a woman and mumbled a stilted "Sorry" before she moved back towards the crush.

"Whoa, hang on," the woman said, keeping hold of Leah's arm. "Are you alright?"

"I'm fine, I—" Leah's vision adjusted, and she jerked in surprise. "You're that woman from the bakery stand. Moonsugar or something."

"That's me," she said. "I don't have my nametag on. I'm Monroe." She laid her other hand on Leah's shoulder, the weight strangely comforting, but it wasn't enough to stem the urge to shift. "Are you sure you're okay?"

"I said I'm fine!" Leah snapped, wrenching away from her and already bathing in the guilt she'd have to unpack later for being so rude. She didn't bother to say anything else, she rushed for the first public bathroom, situated right next to the escalators.

"Everyone out!" Leah barked, though it came out as more of a growl than anything else. One look at her meaty hand sprouting fur, and she backslid into a deep and inexorable panic. "Mandatory cleaning!"

The people in line groaned angrily but dispersed, and though people inside the bathroom weren't actually moving slower than molasses, it felt like that to Leah, who was turned away from the mirrors, not wanting to draw any more attention to what was staring to look more like a muzzle than a face. When the last person exited, she slammed the door, throwing the deadbolt and tearing off her jacket and jeans, followed by the rest. Glancing around at the corners, she was grateful that there weren't any cameras present.

The shift came fast and sharp, tearing into her like a hot knife through butter, rearranging her organs and her skeletal structure one sickening crunch at a time. Her spine sent her to all fours, and she would have vomited her breakfast onto the floor at the thought of touching a public bathroom floor if she hadn't been biting her tongue hard enough to bleed as she tried not to vocalize what was happening.

"Hey in there," a voice said.

"Closed for cleaning!" Leah managed to croak. "Come back later!"

"It's Monroe." There was a quiet shuffling of wet boots against tile on the other side of the door. "I get panic attacks too, sometimes. They used to be worse, you know, much... hairier." She chuckled softly to herself, laughing at her own joke. "What's your name?"

"Leah." It was the last thing she'd be able to say before her face lengthened further, contorting her vocal cords from the lithe flexibility of a human's into the stark horror of a Bear's.

"Hi, Leah. I'm not going to ask to come in, in fact, I'm going to watch the door for you, alright?" Monroe asked, her voice a soothing tone through the door. "I've got your back. Don't worry, okay? You just focus on taking some nice deep breaths."

Leah would have thanked her, but knew the words would come out as a garbled sound, and not words. She huffed, letting the shift sink into her skin, bulking her out until she was almost too big to pace the length of the bathroom. She checked each stall again, knowing they would be empty but needing to check anyway, to cover her tracks, to make sure she wouldn't wind up in the back of some government van on her way to a secret base in the middle of the desert out west.

She breathed in, and breathed out, each exhale taking more of the adrenaline with it. Leah sat back on her haunches, still shaking from the early shift, but finally able to focus her vision and her thoughts toward returning to her usual human form. She waited, eyes shut because if there was anything more horrifying than a shift, it was watching it in ten-foot-long mirrors above a water-splashed countertop. It took nearly fifteen minutes for her to fully de-fur, and when she did, she dressed with shaky hands, her fingers almost too unwieldy for the buttons of her jeans and shirt. She let the jacket hang open.

Unlocking the door, she pulled it open with some trepidation, unsure if Monroe was still there or not.

"Hey," Monroe said, pushing herself off the wall. "I kept a lookout for you, and sent some folks to the other bathroom up towards the department store." She squinted at Leah, her head tilted. "You sure you're alright?"

"Better now," Leah admitted. "Thanks."

Monroe clapped a hand on her shoulder, squeezing gently against the leather. "I'm glad to hear it." She glanced around, nodding towards the escalator. "Upstairs isn't as mobbed."

"That's where I was headed, my—uh—she wants boba tea."

Monroe snorted a quiet laugh, shaking her head in recognition. "Better get her what she wants then," she soothed playfully. "If you head to the back side of the mall upstairs, there's a freight elevator that drops you right next to that candle store on the other side. Might be easier than fighting the crowds, and given how busy it is, no one will fight you." She shrugged. "We did a pop-up here a few weeks ago."

"Yeah, uh… thanks," Leah said, and meant it all the way from her formerly clawed toes. "Happy holidays, Monroe."

"I hope your *uh* becomes what you're hoping for," Monroe said, easing back into the crowd. "Have a nice season, Leah."

Chapter Sixteen

Leah returned to the line with two large boba teas, three bags, and a funnel cake. "Almost in," she said, nodding at the front of the line. "Not too long?"

"I didn't realize you were going to go on a shopping spree," Jasmine said, taking the purple tea. "This right here makes all the drama in the parking lot worth the trip."

"I think I saw a fistfight break out," Leah mused, taking a sip of the drink. It surprised her with the delicate sweetness, underscored by another flavor she couldn't quite pin down. Being able to focus on the taste helped her ease back down to normal, but her skin still prickled with frustration at the surrounding environment. "If you'd said we were looking for one of those talking plushie things, I never would have come. People are ready for bloodshed."

"Good thing we're all boring adults, then." Jasmine craned her neck around the corner, trying to peer inside the store. "I wish I could tell if they have any of the Blackberry Sunrise candles left."

Leah raised up onto her toes, the muscles in her calves taut with the effort. "What does it look like?"

"Purple label." Jasmine pointed at the clear cup in her hand. "Like this."

"I can't see over the giant festive display of peppermint," Leah apologized, lowering herself back down. "We'll just have to wait." She took another sip, allowing the drink to grow on her, and chewed one of the tapioca balls from the straw. "Anyway, I picked up some extra snacks. I felt bad that your Paps and I demolished two bags of chips last night."

"Don't apologize," Jasmine said, bouncing on the balls of her feet. "I'm sure he was just pleased to have a partner in crime. Mom and I go to bed too early for him to break out the midnight feasts." The Candlebath employee waved them both in, stopping the group behind them.

The smell, which had been noticeable beyond the door, was almost too thick to breathe once they were inside. Out of habit, Leah tugged her shirt up over her nose, wishing she'd taken Annie's insistence to wear a scarf along with her jacket. At least it would have helped block some of it out, even if it would only have contributed to her constant overheating. It was a thick, floral scent, somewhere between a funeral home and those huge jugs of syrup for snow cones in the summer. "Do you see the ones you need?" Leah asked.

"Not yet." Jasmine stopped another employee, asking where they could find the candles.

"Uh, we're sold out," the employee mumbled. "Of almost everything. If there are any, they'll be over in that corner."

Leah had seen worse at Syndicorp, but not by far. The shelves were a mess, strewn with products from all over the store, some of them broken or opened, none of them in any sort of order. She set her bags down, starting to go through the assortment of candles, soaps, and sprays one at a time.

"Come on, you don't have to do that," Jasmine said from behind her. "He said they're sold out. We can just go."

"No, he implied there might still be some down here," Leah replied, stacking matching candles against the back wall of the shelf. "It won't take me long to check." The different scents were disparate, thickening the air around them. Her sense of smell was always heightened that close to a moon, and twenty-five minutes after having already shifted, the shop was almost suffocating. Daffodil spring, peaches and cream, ocean breeze, petrichor. A tester spray fell to the ground, leaking shimmery liquid across Leah's jeans. She wiped it off and pushed the bottle to the back, where no one else would slip on it, trying to breathe more through her mouth, as if that would be of any real help.

Leah took a drink of her boba, surprising herself with how much she was enjoying the taste of it. She rarely spent money on anything nonessential, and the festive season was rarely an exception to that self-imposed rule. The sugar gave her just enough of a boost to keep organizing the shelf, looking for their prize.

"Leah," Jasmine said again. "It's not going to be there. We should just go before the streets get too busy with traffic, I'll just have to give her an I-owe—"

"Bam," Leah said, producing candles with the right scent. "I told you."

"You're an angel," Jasmine said, setting both into her empty basket. "I never would have found those."

Leah smirked. "Yeah, that's why you work on cash." She dug into another pile, ferreting out three sample-sized candles and a body wash, piling them into the basket alongside the others. "It takes a special skill set to find things in piles."

"Obviously," Jasmine replied, rearranging the products in the basket. "Got anything else down there?"

"Looks like three, maybe four of those big ones. Three wicks?" Leah said, turning the label to read more. "Crackling wicks?"

Jasmine crouched down alongside her, holding out the basket. "Load them up, Erickson. Those are the holy grail. The favorites. I swear they are never in stock, even when they're in season." She squinted into the darkness beneath the shelf. "I wonder if someone stashed them here."

"If so, it was months ago," Leah responded, wiping a thick layer of dust off the label. "Forgotten and abandoned. Ours now, though." She placed each of them into the basket and stood up, sliding into the crowded line for the cash register.

Jasmine laid a hand on her arm. "Thank you," she said. "Honestly. Mom… I don't know, we have our issues, I guess, but she means well. She just worries too much, and I want her to stop." She adjusted her long knitted scarf, wrapping it around her neck once more to keep the fringe from dragging on the muddy floor. "That's kind of what all this was about."

"I gathered," Leah said, shifting the weight of the basket from one forearm to the other, making sure not to spill her drink. Candles were surprisingly heavy. "So it's this job, right?" she asked. "You want to make sure that if you get an interview, you can just go without too much drama?"

"Something like that." Jasmine sighed, pressing in closer to Leah to allow a frenzied pair to pass them, heading for the same shelf they'd just vacated. "I want her to make more friends. Taking up with the yarn stuff helped a lot, but she needs more of it."

"And you?" Leah asked. "What about your friends, your hobbies?"

"I just want to get the heck out of Rockland Heights," Jasmine replied acerbically. "I feel stagnant here. I'm tired of Syndicorp already, and it's only been a few weeks. One more dead-end job in a string of pointless positions, I get bored and check out, wind up looking for something else before too long."

The line shifted, and they both followed suit. "I'd miss you at work," Leah said, immediately regretting it. "I just mean, I don't have many friends there. Phil is fine, but he can be annoying."

"Phil never collects his re-shop," Jasmine sniped. "I wind up having to do it for him in the morning before opening." She swallowed back a sharp snort of a laugh, setting her basket on the counter. "Plus, two weeks ago, he ate my sandwich out of the staff fridge."

"I retract my statement," Leah said. "Phil is clearly a monster."

"He's basically irredeemable," Jasmine agreed. The cashier scanned each of the items, wrapping the fragile glass in brown paper before setting them into a matching bag, the jute handles prepared for the weight.

Leah reached out and took the bag as Jasmine paid, holding it with the rest of her bags.

"You don't have to carry that," Jasmine said, reaching for it.

"It's fine," Leah said, gently swerving out of her reach. "I don't mind."

"What are you, some knight in shining armor?" Jasmine asked, jokingly nudging Leah in the arm.

Leah tilted her head, unsure of the strange dynamic they'd cultivated. "If you'd let me," she said. They didn't have time to consider her words, or where precisely they laid on a scale between joking around and sincerity, because they were already being dragged to the store's entrance just with the flow of traffic around the tables. She knew what she meant, but not if Jasmine would accept it or not. Looking back at Jasmine's settled, determined face, Leah couldn't even tell if Jasmine had even heard her in the first place. The store was loud, after all, with the chatter of customers, pressed down by the noisy covers of carols piped in over the speakers. Leah's skin rippled again, and she breathed with intent, willing herself to calm back to a normal level.

"I guess that's everything," Jasmine said, draining the rest of her drink along with the tapioca balls at the bottom. "We can probably head back now."

"No more last-minute shopping?" Leah prompted. "Nothing for your Paps?"

Jasmine shook her head. "Nah, Mom and I went in on something together for him. We've had it for months under her bed." She led the way through the thick press of people, reaching back to grab for Leah's hand.

Leah shifted the bags and drink to one fist in order to interlace her fingers with Jasmine's, a motion that already felt so casually normal that it was dangerous for when their scheme was all over. She hoped that Jasmine didn't notice how sweaty her palms were. "We can share the funnel cake in the car," she suggested. "It's in that yellow bag there."

"Sharing is caring," Jasmine parroted, on auto-pilot as they navigated their way out of the increasingly busy mall. Pushing the door, the cold air slammed into Leah like a life-giving breath, freeing her from the stagnant, recycled atmosphere from inside. Cars were lining both sides of each parking lot aisle, all of them waiting for a spot.

Every car they passed stared at them, willing them to stop sooner, to offer them a free parking space, and it felt like being on display at a fish market, with many pairs of greedy eyes just waiting to pounce. "I bet you could offer your space to someone for fifty bucks and they'd pay it," Leah mused.

"How magnanimous of you," Jasmine replied, already digging her keys out of her pocket. "Personally, I'd rather not wind up the subject of some anonymous internet messaging board, no matter how intense the parking is right now." She unlocked the car, and as the lights flashed, no fewer than three cars moved into position to jockey for the space.

"We should hurry," Leah urged, setting the bags on the back seat and jumping into the passenger side in two swift movements. "Or any of them might get a little intense."

"They can wait," Jasmine said, buckling her seat belt and checking her mirrors. "I'm not about to get into a fender bender because these fools can't relax for half a second."

One of the cars honked, the driver showing off a rude gesture. Anger flared beneath Leah's skin, and she swallowed back the retort that bubbled in her throat, edging dangerously close to a low growl. He was yelling something, but with all the windows closed, she couldn't tell what it was, and the Bear within her was itching for a fight after being caged in the bathroom for fifteen excruciatingly long minutes.

Leah adjusted her seat, the manual latch difficult to see in the fading light. "Jazz, are you ready?"

"Yeah, just a minute," Jasmine said, turning on the lights and the radio, turning down the volume. "Okay, let's go."

"Hey!" the driver said, now leaning out of his window. "Are you two going to move your asses, or what?"

Leah flung off her belt, practically leaping out of the car. She couldn't hold back any longer, not without risking another ill-timed shift. "What did you say?" she demanded.

"I said move!" he replied, but the flash of fear in his eyes made him prey to her predator.

"Leah, get back in the car!" Jasmine shouted, pleading as she reached for her door handle.

Leah put a hand up to stop Jasmine in her tracks and continued to advance on the truck. "Do we have a problem?" she asked, staring through his window, resisting the urge to break through the glass and let her meaty paw drag claws through his leather seats.

"Are you going to camp in that space all day?" he shot back, but wouldn't hold eye contact with her. "Some people have lives, you know."

"And if you had waited another ten seconds, we would have." She leaned against the truck, bracing on her forearms, the metal zip tapping against the immaculate paint job. "Tomorrow is Christmas, sir, so if I were you, I'd drive away right now and hope I wasn't visited by a few ghosts tonight."

"Are you threatening me?" he retorted, finally brave enough to meet her stare. "I'm twice your size, little lady. You won't like how things end if they come to blows."

The moon hadn't even risen yet, but the shift rippled beneath Leah's skin. "Trust me, pal, I've taken on bigger men than you, and they've all cried like newborns." She stepped back, showing off a casual shrug. "You should go."

He mumbled a curse under his breath but put his truck into gear and began backing up the aisle. Leah smiled at the woman in the adjacent car, motioning for her to take their spot when they pulled out. The third car had found another spot in the adjacent column, preferring to stay out of the confrontation entirely. The woman smiled, waving in thanks.

"Leah, what the hell?" Jasmine asked when she got back into the car.

"What?" Leah asked, more sharply than she'd intended. It had been a long time since she'd lost her composure like that, and it hung in the air like silt.

"He could have gotten out of his truck, could have thrown a punch or something, or worse," Jasmine warned. "I don't understand why you would do that over a parking space."

"I don't like when people are rude," Leah answered simply, trying to seem normal even as she fought her pulse. "And he was rude."

"I'm not so sure I want to drive to either the emergency room or the police station today, so maybe we can keep the reckless behavior to a minimum?" Jasmine started the car, pulling out of the spot. "He was way bigger than either of us."

"I told you, cycles are hard for me," Leah said, hoping that would be enough and knowing it wouldn't be. "I'm not usually that confrontational."

"I hope not," Jasmine replied, her voice oddly hollow and devoid of its usual warmth.

"Should we pick up anything for dinner?" Leah asked, desperate to shift back into their usual easy conversation.

Jasmine glanced at her from the corner of her eye as she pulled out into traffic. "Text my mom from my phone," she responded after a long moment. "The passcode is one-two-three-four."

"That's the worst passcode I've ever heard," Leah said, tapping it in. "Oh, she already texted. She said to bring back some fried chicken."

Jasmine nodded thoughtfully, her brow still furrowed, her mouth still pressed into a thin line. "Yeah."

"Okay," Leah said evenly, but as she sank back into her seat, couldn't help but worry that she'd ruined everything before it had even really started.

Chapter Seventeen

"Hey, we're back," Jasmine announced, locking the door behind them. She took the bags from Leah and traded her the sacks of food, nodding towards the kitchen. "I'll hide the stuff," she whispered. "You can just unload all of that onto the island."

Leah nodded, somehow holding both the sacks of chicken and the cardboard drink holders at once.

"Hello," Jasmine called into the living room, finding it empty. She took the stairs two at a time, angling to stash the candles in her closet to wrap later that night. "Anybody home?" she asked. Her mother's car was still out front, so it seemed unlikely that they'd left.

"Hey, Jazzy," her grandpa said, meeting her at her bedroom door. "Did you get the stuff?"

"Yeah, I got the stuff," she replied, holding the bag aloft. "Plenty of it. Want me to wrap for you?"

He nodded. "I'll trade you for that last muffin I called dibs on."

"Deal." She set the bags down inside her closet, sliding the mirrored door closed. "Where's Mom?"

"Garage. Told me to keep out." He shrugged and then stretched his arms over his head with an exaggerated yawn. "That was some nap I had."

"Glad you enjoyed yourself. The mall was packed and some guy who wanted our space got all aggressive." Jasmine hung up her parka, sliding her feet into her tall slippers.

Her grandpa stood straight, squaring his shoulders. "Are you okay?" he demanded, but kindly. "What happened?"

Jasmine fixed her hair in the mirror, tying it up into a high bun. "Leah scared him off," she answered. She still wasn't sure how she felt about that interaction, in part because it was dangerous, and in part because Leah's display of aggression didn't sit well in her gut.

"You know how some people get around the holidays, Jazz," he mused. "They set up all kinds of pressure for themselves and then can't handle it when the chickens come home to roost."

"I would prefer not having shouting matches in parking lots," Jasmine muttered. "We picked up chicken. Mom said to."

Her grandpa threw off a devious grin. "That was me. She left her phone on the counter, unlocked."

"You're going to regret that one of these days," Jasmine warned.

He extended his arms, pulling her in for an embrace. "I didn't even look at anything, I only replied to your text from earlier asking if we needed anything else."

"Mmhmm," Jasmine replied, doubting that he hadn't been creeping around looking for hints about what they'd gotten him for Christmas. "Leah is setting the food out downstairs if you want to help."

"You know, Jazz..." he trailed off, tightening his silvery ponytail.

"What?" she prompted.

He searched her face for something and then pulled her into an embrace. "I just want you to be happy, you know that, right? Your mom, too."

Jasmine patted him on the back before escaping the hug, ducking out from under his arms to close her bedroom door against prying eyes. "I know," she replied, tugging on the slippers she'd taken from beneath her bed. "You don't have to tell me."

"Any news about this interview?" he asked, leaning against the railing's post. "I think that if you get an interview, you'll dazzle them."

"I doubt I'll hear anything until after Christmas," she demurred, eager to leave the topic behind, at least for a few more days. "You know how it is."

He glanced around, making sure that they were alone upstairs. "I have a little stashed away, Jazz. If you get this job, it's yours to help you find a place.

It's not much, it's not buy-a-house money, but it might be first and last and security deposit money." He inhaled deeply, blowing it out immediately as a forlorn sigh. "I'd miss your face around these parts, of course, but I know you have to make your own way. Your mom knows, too, she's just…"

"Yeah," Jasmine affirmed, rubbing the toe of her slipper into the rug, catching the fringe at the edges. "I know." She hugged him again, this time letting it linger just a moment longer. "Thanks, Paps," she said. "I don't know if anything will come of this, but it's nice to know that you have my back."

"I'm sorry it's not more." He released her, his hands still on her shoulders. "Your grandma and I, we worked hard, but it wasn't enough to leave much. And your dad…"

Jasmine tensed, and he noticed.

"Sorry," he said quickly, shoving his hands into his pockets. "Sore subject."

"Can we do this later?" she asked. "I don't want the food to get cold. It's freezing out there, even with the car's heater on full blast." She rubbed her hands together for emphasis, tugging the sleeves of her sweater down over her thumbs. "Thank you, really, I just… can't think about this right now."

He nodded, taking his glasses and folding them into his t-shirt pocket. "I just wanted you to know that you can be honest with me. And with your mom, for that matter. I know things are rocky sometimes, but she's getting there, you know."

"I know," Jasmine replied, turning back towards the stairs. "Come on, Paps, I'm hungry."

"Did you get the gravy?" he asked, footsteps directly behind hers. "That's the best part, you know."

"Leah ordered double." She turned, flashing him a grin. "Looks like you found your perfect match when it comes to fried chicken."

"And have you?" he whispered, leaning forward into her ear. "Found your perfect match?"

"I'd push you, but we're on the stairs and you might break a hip." Jasmine leaped down the last three steps, leaving his question unanswered. His invasiveness wasn't unusual, he was just as overprotective as her mother, he just showed it differently. Despite the intention, it still felt like the walls were closing in when they both hammered her with questions. "Hey," she said loudly, hoping that would discourage any more interrogations. "Thanks for getting started."

"Has the treasure been buried?" Leah asked, taking a bucket of chicken out of the bag. "Does X mark the spot?"

"What are we, pirates?" Jasmine retorted, laughing. "But yes." She went to the garage door, shouting through it. "Mom, we're back and Paps is going to eat all the chicken! You'd better finish whatever you're working on and get in here!"

"Just finishing some work," her mother replied amidst the sound of something crashing into the concrete flooring. "It has to be ready for the twenty-eighth."

Leah folded down the empty paper bags and turned in a circle, looking for plates.

"In there," Jasmine directed, pointing at one of the hanging cabinets. "Third shelf. Paps!" she called. "I thought you were going to help Leah!"

"I am, I am," he defended, sauntering into the kitchen. "I was turning on the lights." He collected the silverware, piling it on the island next to the plates. "Annie!" he shouted. "Annie, I'm going to devour every drumstick!"

The door creaked open, and Jasmine's mother eased through, closing it behind her before anyone could see what she'd been working on. "You'd better not, Dad," she warned, snatching a piece of chicken from the bucket. "It's Christmas Eve, behave yourself."

"What are you working on?" he asked, nonchalant but with that pervasive undercurrent of nosiness. "Is it for me?"

"No, you old goat, it's for work," her mother protested. "Your gift has been cleverly hidden away somewhere you'll never find it, no matter how many loads of laundry you spontaneously decide to kindly hang in my closet for me." She raised an eyebrow as she filled her plate with mashed potatoes, biscuits, chicken, gravy, and green beans. "You forget that your granddaughter is just as crafty as you. I've had better hiding spots for years."

"And you forget that I've lived here longer, and know all of them," he boasted.

Jasmine snorted a laugh, taking the large spoon from her mother. "Yet you haven't found it yet," she countered. "Curious." She took what she wanted and handed the spoon to Leah, heading to the kitchen table to eat. "The mall was absolutely packed, by the way. Never doing that again."

"What's the matter, did you encounter all of the other last-minute shoppers?" Her mother gave her a wry smile as she dunked her chicken into the gravy. "Maybe next year you'll be more organized."

"I'm plenty organized, thank you, it's certain other members of this household who aren't." Jasmine sat down across from her mother, leaving the seat next to her free for Leah to take. "I left your change for dinner on the counter," she said, loading up a forkful of potatoes and gravy. "Movie tonight?"

"Pajama party," her mother replied. "Leah, you don't have to if you don't want to, it's just our little tradition."

"I have pajamas," Leah confirmed, her plate already almost empty. "I love a pajama party. It's been years since I've gone to one." She sopped up gravy with a biscuit, shoving it into her mouth. "What movie?"

"My favorite," Jasmine's grandfather insisted, pouring more gravy onto his plate, creating a savory lake that flowed from potatoes to green beans. "It might be old, but it's a classic."

***

The movie was already queued up and waiting when they piled into the living room, all of them in their pajamas. Jasmine was grateful to change into something softer and elasticated after a day in skinny jeans, her festive-printed leggings soft and cozy, tucked into her slippers. Her oversized, long-sleeved shirt was an old one from college, the collar floppy, the cuffs frayed and threadbare. Despite all that, it was a favorite.

"Are we ready?" her grandfather asked, settling into the wingback chair with the remote. His thick, fleece pajama pants were a dark blue, almost navy, one of his gifts from the previous Christmas.

Leah adjusted her position on the sofa, allowing more room for Jasmine. "I'm ready," she confirmed. "Jazz, you can stretch out, if you want." She held up a thick, knitted blanket, the cables bulky but evenly stitched. "Are you cold?"

"Yeah, a little," Jasmine admitted, scooting in close to her to share the blanket. As always, Leah was warm, like a hot water bottle or a heating pad, and Jasmine couldn't resist the temptation to snuggle in closer.

"Dad, I got those things you like," her mother said, depositing a large bowl of lentil chips on the coffee table along with a large tub of sour cream and onion dip. "You have to share, though."

"I always share!" he protested, already leaning forward to reach for a handful of chips. "Leah and I shared chips last night, in fact, I let her finish them off."

"Don't throw our guest under the snack bus," Jasmine's mother chided, crossing her legs beneath her as she sank into a bean bag chair. "I know you, and I know your ways."

"Alright already," Jasmine interrupted, snacking on a chip despite her full stomach. "Start the movie before we eat through all the food." She handed one to Leah, loaded with dip.

"Thanks," Leah said with a cute grin, popping it into her mouth. She stretched her arms over her head, landing with one around Jasmine's shoulders, gently encouraging her to come closer.

Jasmine obliged, leaning her head against Leah's shoulder, settling the blanket over both of them equally. "Let me know if you get too warm," she whispered.

"I'm fine," Leah replied, reaching for another chip. "I'll let you know."

"I'm pressing play now," Jasmine's grandfather announced, holding the remote aloft like it was a trophy. The intro credits played in black and white, the music swelling as it crescendoed over the speakers.

It was a familiar film, and a comforting one. Jasmine started to doze, and Leah just pulled her closer. It was an oddly safe feeling, like being wrapped in a chrysalis, just waiting to burst forth when the time was right. For the moment, she was happy to watch an old film with her family, and to pretend that the fiction she and Leah had cooked up was real.

She'd be gone the day after the next, and they'd go back to just being co-workers. If Jasmine's luck was ripe, maybe not even that for much longer. Anxiety over the potential interview probed at her, its thorns gripping around the base of her skull.

"What's wrong?" Leah whispered in her ear. "Are you okay?"

Jasmine nodded, sinking further down into the couch until her head rested in Leah's lap. The film played on, a story of gratefulness and civic responsibility that lit a matchstick of hope in her heart, a rarity the older she got. She tried to focus on the movie, challenging herself to pay attention to the cinematography, the sets, even the costumes, because that was easier than the constant consideration of her potentially bleak and uninteresting future.

"Shh," Leah whispered, playing with Jasmine's hair.

There was something so casually familiar about it that Jasmine nearly bolted upright, almost pushed Leah's hand away, or scolded her to stop, but she didn't. Instead, she breathed out a quiet sigh and leaned into the touch, the first she'd had of that kind since Danielle and sorely missed.

Jasmine took the scrunchie from her hair, letting it fall loose over Leah's lap. She craved more, but couldn't quite bring herself to ask for it. Beneath the blanket, she looked for a place to rest her hand, mistakenly laying it on Leah's knee before relocating to hug herself, instead.

"Intermission!" her grandfather shouted, pausing the movie. "Old man needs to use the little boy's room. Does anyone want anything while I'm up?" he asked, eyeing up the now-empty bag of chips. "More snacks?" He wiggled his eyebrows at Leah. "How about you, midnight snack pal?"

"Martin, it's barely nine in the evening," Leah protested, laughing. "But if you put food in front of me, I will probably eat it."

He grinned, practically dancing out of the room. "Stand by," he said. "Also, now is the time for anyone to stretch or re-acclimate themselves." He glared playfully at Jasmine's mother. "Annie, that means you."

"What are you talking about?" she retorted. "I'm just sitting here, minding my own business."

"For once," Jasmine supplied, burying her laugh in the blanket. "I'm kidding, Mom, don't give me that look."

Her grandfather poked his head back into the living room. "Annie, I love you, but you always wait until I'm back to decide you need something."

"I'm fine, Dad," she grumbled. "What about you two? Bathroom break?" She narrowed her eyes at Leah. "Smoke break?"

"I don't smoke," Leah replied. "Never have. And I'm okay, but thank you."

Jasmine's grandfather reappeared with a tray of treats, foil-wrapped chocolates from some secret stash somewhere, a fresh pack of cookies, four cans of soda, some honey-roasted peanuts, and a jar of pickles.

"Pickles?" Leah asked, snagging one of the cans and opening the top with a noisy hiss of carbonation.

"Trust me," he replied. "It cuts the sweetness."

Jasmine nestled into the blanket, not interested in snacks or soda because she was still full from dinner and chips. The movie played on, the music warm and familiar, and before she knew it, her eyelids were growing heavy with sleep.

Chapter Eighteen

Leah hadn't woken up early on Christmas morning since she was a young child, maybe six years old, before she learned that the whole thing was a sham to get people to spend more money than they could afford. And yet, she lay awake on the floor, staring up at the white textured ceiling, counting the swirls in the pattern. She checked her phone again for the fourteenth time, willing the minutes to pass faster. Staying there was only complicating matters, and the impending full moon was making her antsy, like razorblades under her skin.

It was only eight in the morning, the sun only just risen. She tugged the blankets up to her chin. She might run hot, but the temperatures outside had fallen quickly, setting a chill on the house that was far more noticeable on the hardwood floor, protected only by a latch hook rug and the spare blanket from the linen closet.

Scrolling through the apps on her phone, she huffed out a frustrated breath and tossed it aside. There was nothing worth seeing on there, and nothing worth doing, either. She was almost starting to look forward to that month's shift. Being a Bear in the heat of summer was miserable, all covered in fur and no way to escape it. Winter was freedom for a Bear, the woods were emptier, and she was left alone. It was easier to hide food caches undisturbed, too.

A soft knock on the door roused her into full consciousness, and panic gripped her. "Jasmine," she hissed, tugging on the quilt. "Jazz!"

"Good morning, Merry Christmas!" Annie sang through the door. "I hope you girls are ready for breakfast, Martin is making French toast!"

Leah tugged harder on the blankets, almost pulling them off. "Jasmine!"

"Hmm?" Jasmine opened one eye, and then the other. "Hey," she said, yawning.

"Your mother," Leah mouthed, jabbing a thumb in the direction of the door.

Jasmine bolted up in bed, adjusting the quilt. "Uh, hi Mom," she said, her voice still gravelly with sleep. "Merry Christmas."

"Can I come in?" Annie asked, jiggling the door knob. "I assume you're both decent, seeing as Jazzy conked out on the couch last night."

"Uh—" Jasmine started, motioning for Leah to join her in the bed. "One second."

Leah jumped into the bed, wrapping an arm around Jasmine's shoulders. "Morning!" she chirped, right as Annie opened the door.

"Well, aren't you both all bright-eyed and bushy-tailed?" Annie said with a playful smirk. "Good to see you're both awake. Jazzy, Paps is cooking breakfast. Are you hungry?"

"Uh, sure," Leah replied, doing her best to not look at the pile of blankets she'd left in full view. She should have kicked them under the bed, but she hadn't in her panic. Despite being awake for at least an hour by then, she was still acting like she was half-asleep.

"French toast?" Annie repeated. "Is that okay with you, Leah?"

"Sounds great!" Leah croaked, her voice cracking with anxiety. "I mean, yes, please, that sounds incredible." Her stomach growled loudly, as if to punctuate her point.

Annie laughed, waving a hand at them both. "Alright, I'll tell him. The bathroom is free for anyone who needs it, we're all good out here." She went to close the door, pausing just long enough to spot the blankets on the floor. Thankfully, she said nothing, latching it instead.

"That was a close one," Jasmine muttered, throwing off the quilt. "Sorry. She's a little overly exuberant on Christmas."

Leah followed suit, gathering her clothes for the day. "I think she saw the blankets," she whispered, draping jeans and a fresh shirt over her arm. "Do you think she'll know?"

"I don't know," Jasmine answered, and then cursed under her breath. "I'm sorry, I'm such a heavy sleeper. I didn't even hear her at first. It's a good thing you were already awake." She paused at her closet, hands hovering over the handle as she caught Leah's eye in the mirror. "Couldn't sleep?"

"Something like that," Leah replied, pulling on her jeans. "It happens sometimes."

Jasmine slid open the closet door, groaning at the sight of the bags at the bottom. "I forgot to wrap these, and I need to shower."

"I'll do it," Leah offered. "I used to work at a home goods store, I had to learn how to gift wrap." She held her arms out, waiting for the candles. "Go shower, I've got this."

"Are you sure?" Jasmine's face contorted with suspicion and concern, her brow furrowed and her full lips pouty. "It doesn't seem fair."

"All part of the deal," Leah assured her, twitching her fingers. "Come on. Hand it over."

Jasmine set the bags on the bed, along with a fresh roll of brown paper and some wide-wired ribbon from a basket under the bed. "Paps won't let us use anything that you can't recycle," she explained, gesturing at the brown paper. "And most of it can't be."

"Too bad our customers at Syndicorp don't care about that," Leah mused. "It would make reorganizing the seasonal aisle a lot easier."

"You've got that right," Jasmine agreed, choking on a laugh. "You're sure this is okay? I can do it when I get out, if you—"

Leah pointed at the door, already rolling out the wrapping paper on the floor. "Go!" she insisted. Before the lock even latched, she was already cutting out the correct shapes and amounts for each of the candles, choosing to bundle the smaller ones together. The paper was thick and hearty, perfect for sharp creases. She folded ribbon around each package, tying large, show-stopper bows, just like she had at her job. It was strangely soothing, returning to such quiet, methodical work. She found herself wishing she could have run the gift-wrap desk from behind a privacy screen, instead of having to make small talk with customers as they watched her work, eagle-eyed for any mistakes.

By the time Jasmine scrambled back through the door, tugging a brush through her freshly washed and dried hair, Leah was sitting back on the bed, again scrolling through her phone, the packages wrapped and labeled next to the trunk. "All done?" Leah asked casually, knowing she'd done a good job.

"These look incredible," Jasmine said, inspecting each package. "My mom is going to know it was you, my wrapping is terrible. Usually, I just crumple a bunch of paper and tie it up with ribbon."

"Breakfast?" Leah prompted, gathering the gifts into her arms. As Jasmine nodded, she started down the stairs, stopping in the living room to arrange the presents under the tree. Outside, the sun shone down on freshly fallen snow, sparkling painfully in the light. Still, cold crept under the front door, an icy draft not defeated by the long knitted snake that lay along the inside mat.

"Merry Christmas!" Martin shouted, holding a spatula aloft. "Leah, I hope you like eggnog."

"I love it," Leah confirmed, perching on one of the stools at the island. "Can I help?"

"No!" he shouted, laughing in a conspiratorial manner. "No helping. This is all me. Later it will be Annie, but for now, I am the reigning regent of the kitchen." He turned and flipped a piece in the air, catching it in the cast-iron pan. "Syrup or powdered sugar?" he asked. "We have strawberries I think, unless Annie ate them all."

"I didn't eat them all," Annie retorted, pushing away the bowl in front of her. "Jazzy doesn't even like strawberries, does she, Leah?"

"Uh, no," Leah said, already out of her depth. She scooted the stool closer, willing Jasmine to come and save her from the inquisition. "I like syrup as long as it's maple," she answered. "But I won't say no to powdered sugar either."

Martin slid three thick pieces of French toast onto a plate and pushed it across the tiles. "Syrup and fixings are on the table," he said. "Juice is in the jug, freshly squeezed. Bacon is coming up."

"Wow, a feast," Leah said, taking the plate. "I don't know how I'll manage to eat later, too." She took her food to the table and sat down, drowning it in syrup. The scent of the maple mixed with the spiced eggnog clouded her brain, and all she was thinking about was keeping up her strength for the following night's shift. With the cold being so vicious, she'd need it.

"We don't eat until at least four," Annie supplied, stealing another strawberry from the bowl. "Trust me, we'll all be ready to pack our plates full. We have turkey, ham, a lasagna, green bean casserole, mashed potatoes, cauliflower and cheese, glazed carrots, and cheesecake for dessert."

Jasmine stopped at the stove to hug her grandfather. "Mom, you know there are only four of us, right?"

"I want leftovers!" Annie argued. "Every year we have plans for leftovers, and every year it looks like a swarm of locusts buzzed through the kitchen, so this year I'm coming prepared." She shielded her eyes against the bright glare of the snow, squinting into the window. "Good thing no one is driving today, you'd wind up snow-blind. That's if you even got the cars to start, it's so darn cold."

Leah loaded up her fork and took a bite, the taste perfection in her mouth. The toast was perfect, with gently crispy edges and a softer center, soaked overnight in spiced eggnog and slathered with butter as soon as it came out of the pan. It was perfect. "Martin, this is delicious," she said between mouthfuls. "I don't think I've ever had a more decadent Christmas morning breakfast."

He grinned, clearly pleased with his culinary prowess. "Jazz, you need to invite Leah for every holiday, okay? My ego needs it."

"Your ego is just fine, I think," Jasmine replied with a snort. She sat next to Leah and reached across her for the juice. "Sorry, honey," she apologized, flashing a smile.

Leah nudged the juice closer, growing uncomfortable with their charade. At times it felt shallow and exactly what they'd agreed upon, but other times, it was too real, sinking into her chest with a dangerous warmth. "Pour me some, please," she asked.

"I saw presents under the tree," Jasmine said, filling both of their glasses. "Looks like Santa came last night."

Her mother glanced up, her eyebrows knitted together. "Oh, really? I thought maybe he'd forgotten this year."

"Santa never forgets, and neither do I." Jasmine sliced into her breakfast with the side of her fork and doused it with powdered sugar and strawberries. "Sheesh, Mom, did you have to eat most of them?"

Leah stared down at her plate, hoping she hadn't given away their game. She'd always been good at spotting when things were starting to unravel, and the frayed threads had already begun to appear.

"Are you okay?" Jasmine asked, poking Leah in the arm. "You're quiet."

Leah nodded, answering by shoving another enormous bite into her mouth. It was easier and safer than being truthful. "It's good," she mumbled.

"Hurry, hurry," Martin said, shoveling down his breakfast. "Presents next!"

"You're worse than a kid," Annie chastised, laughing. "You were always up before me, even when I was little."

"Meanwhile your own was up at the crack of dawn when she was a kiddo," Martin said, nodding towards Jasmine. "What was the earliest?"

Annie groaned, stealing a strawberry from Jasmine's plate. "Five in the morning," she said. "It was still pitch black outside, but there was no getting her back to bed, not once she'd seen the presents under the tree. I think Dean and I got about two hours of sleep between us that year." Her face darkened, and she put the strawberry back. "It was a long time ago."

"Dad wasn't even the one who put my bike together, it was you," Jasmine offered, giving her back the strawberry. "Best bike ever. I rode that thing until the wheels fell off." She nudged her mother under the table with her slipper, prompting her to reply. "Come on, Mom," Jasmine pleaded softly. "We shouldn't do this, not today."

Annie brightened, painting on a smile. "You're right," she conceded. "Besides, Leah doesn't need to hear all this." She was staring across the table, Leah could feel Annie's glare boring into her even as she continued to avoid eye contact. "Not when this is only the first time she's spent time with us, right?"

"Mom," Jasmine warned, "don't." She collected their plates, scraping the scraps into the composting bin under the sink. "Leah knows all about it, but it's Christmas, so can we all please chill out?"

"Mm," Annie replied, tempering whatever it was she really wanted to say. "Orange juice, anyone?" Without waiting for a reply, she refilled everyone's glass at the table until the jug was empty. "Thanks for breakfast, Dad. Now you'll have to relinquish the kitchen for the rest of the day."

Martin beamed, leaning back in his chair, the wood squeaking with the effort. "I must say, it was better than last year's sad attempt at festive overnight oats."

"Yeah, please never make that again," Jasmine said over the sound of the tap. "I don't think I'll ever recover from how much cinnamon was in that."

Leah jumped up from her seat, finally awake enough to clock that Jasmine was washing the dishes. "I'll do that," she offered, dunking her hands into the steaming suds.

"No, you're my guest," Jasmine argued, bumping her out of the way with a jut of her hip. "Go sit down, I'll be done in a minute."

"I insist," Leah said, immovable. "Please let me do the dishes, it's the least I can do after everyone's wonderful hospitality."

"Don't get used to it!" Martin chattered gleefully. "Next time we'll revoke your guest pass and put you to work. How do you feel about building raised beds in the spring? Annie has been wanting some for years. Are you good with a saw?"

"Good enough," Leah replied, nudging Jasmine out of the way. "I've never lost a finger, let's put it that way."

Martin was already dragging Annie and Jasmine into the living room, steering them both by the shoulders. "Presents, presents," he sang. "Leah, leave those to soak, the syrup is murder to scrub."

She didn't want to abandon the chore—after all, washing sticky plates was easier than dodging questions and what felt like truth traps set by Jasmine's family. It had been easier when they were watching movies, or at a festival, anything other than staring each other in the face for hours on end. Guilt twisted in her gut, and she wasn't sure whether it was the shame or the oncoming shift that rode the wave of nausea that crested up from too many pieces of French toast.

Morning sunlight gleamed through the large bay window, catching prisms from the carved clear crystals that hung from the top. Leah hadn't seen them before, but they spread wide rainbows across the hardwood floor and the couch alike.

"One for each to start," Annie said, passing out gifts to all of them, sitting back in the bean bag with one that Leah had wrapped that morning. "This one is gorgeous. Jazz, did you wrap this?"

Jasmine shook her head. "It was Leah."

The presence of the gift in her lap was shooting tendrils of panic through Leah's veins. She hadn't participated in the correct exchange, she'd missed the cues, and now she had a gift from Jasmine's mother with nothing to give her in return. "I'm sorry," she said softly, "I didn't bring anything for you, I didn't think, I—"

"It's alright, Leah," Annie soothed. "That's not how things are here. Besides, my dad seems to think you'll be building me some raised beds in the spring? Let's call that an I-owe-you." She winked to punctuate her point, and for half a second, Leah felt like maybe she might be able to relax for the day.

Jasmine's gift was an oversized pullover, hand-knitted with a delicate texture in a yarn that swirled bright pops of color across the torso. "I love it, Mom," she said, swapping it with the sweater she was already wearing. Martin's was similar, but cabled in a deep hunter green with flecks of tweed. He put his on as well, beaming with pride.

Annie delicately slid a finger under the wrapping paper, loosening the tape. "My favorite!" she squealed, setting one of the large candles on the table. "They never have these in stock!"

"Leah found it," Jasmine interjected. "The store said there weren't any."

"Well, thank you to all of you, then," Annie said, folding the paper in order to reuse it later. "And Leah, what beautiful wrapping! You'll have to teach me how you get those creases so perfect." She nodded at her with encouragement. "Now you!"

With considerable trepidation, Leah tore open one side of the package, horrified at what it contained. "Socks," she said, her throat thick with emotion.

"I'm sorry, Jazz didn't give me enough notice for a sweater," Annie apologized. "Maybe next year, if you—well, maybe next year."

"They're beautiful," Leah said, admiring each stitch. The yarn was patterned into stripes and chevrons, alternating shades of scarlet red and a taupe that reminded her of a robin. "I love them." She tugged off a slipper, showing that she had on insulated boot socks. "Great for work or hiking. No blisters." She pocketed the socks she'd been wearing and pulled on the new ones, the fabric so soft against her feet. "Wow, it's like they know what temperature I want to be."

"Don't get her started," Jasmine said with a laugh. "If she waxes poetic about knitting, we won't be eating dinner until at least eight tonight." Jasmine tossed another gift at her grandfather. "You next, Paps."

Chapter Nineteen

Jasmine collected the strewn paper, tucking it into the recycling bag as she picked off the tape. "What do you think, Paps?" she asked, glancing over at his pile of gifts.

"I didn't expect this," he said with awe and a little bit of irritation. "You shouldn't have spent so much on me." He ran his hands over the new rock tumbler, this one larger with more features. "Leah, you'll have to come over to try it out with me."

Jasmine snorted a laugh. "Don't drag her into your old man hobbies, Paps," she chided. "Leah has better things to do than to look at rocks."

Her grandfather tilted his head at her, his brow furrowed. "I would have thought a geologist would have *nothing* better to do than look at rocks," he said slowly. "But perhaps I have misjudged the situation."

"I'd love to," Leah piped up, shooting Jasmine a silencing glare. "I wonder if we can get some really cool stuff to put in there. How do you feel about petrified wood? Or maybe some hematite?" She handed Jasmine more paper from under the sofa. "I know you said you like opalite, I bet some of the secret geologist suppliers have some nice big pieces."

"My grandmother loved opalite," Jasmine said, setting the bag on the ground and taking her seat next to Leah on the couch. "She said she didn't care if they weren't real moonstones."

"Yeah, your Paps said," Leah replied. There was a note of panic on her face that Jasmine couldn't quite track, having no idea where it had originated. "Anyway, there's one gift left under the tree."

Jasmine shook her head fervently, not enjoying where the moment was headed. "No, Leah, you shouldn't have," she protested. "I didn't get you anything, I thought we said no presents this year." She threw Leah a pointed stare. "We agreed."

"I know, but I saw it and just... wanted to get it for you." Leah crawled under the tree, retrieving the final gift, small and thin, but rectangular, and wrapped beautifully, with a large, multi-layered bow gracing the front. "It's nothing special. Don't be mad."

Jasmine pursed her lips together as she took the package, unsticking the bow first and setting it with the rest of the wrapping to be stored and reused for the next year. Inside was a sturdy white box, printed with the name of her favorite notebook brand. "No," she whispered, sliding the drawer from the box. It revealed a perfect, teal, leather-bound journal, complete with three matching ribbons sewn in at the spine. "How did you know?" she asked quietly.

Leah shrugged. "I try to pay attention."

"There's a pencil, too?" Jasmine asked, the weight of it pleasing in her palm. It matched the journal, fitting into a groove at the side of the binding with a small elastic hook to keep it in place.

"I thought it could be for your new job, if you get it." Leah reached out with a hand to touch it, but withdrew, letting it fall into her lap instead. "I hear archivists like to take notes, but never in pen."

"Yeah," Jasmine replied, tears gathering in the corners of her eyes because it was never supposed to be like that. There were never supposed to be any feelings, and there she was, drowning in them, when no matter what happened, their con-woman partnership was nearly at an end. Leah would be leaving first thing in the morning. "Thank you."

Her grandfather sniffled softly, hiding his emotions by blowing his nose into the handkerchief he always kept in his left pocket. He had half a dozen of them, all embroidered with her grandmother's initials. "I love Christmas," he said. "Annie, do you need help in the kitchen?"

"Not from you," Jasmine's mother said playfully, getting up off the bean bag chair. "Last year, you almost burned the green bean casserole."

"It's not my fault the oven runs hot," he grumbled.

"Jazzy, do you want to help?" she asked, tying her cardigan around her waist. "Most is done, really, we just have to babysit some stuff. Leah and Paps can maybe pick a movie for later, what do you think?"

Leah nodded, handing the remote over to Jasmine's grandfather. "I'm kind of a disaster in the kitchen," she admitted. "My skills are embarrassingly limited. I don't cook much with so many housemates."

"I'll be back," Jasmine said, laying a hand on Leah's shoulder as she passed. "Don't let him pick anything weird. Mom hates it when he picks weird stuff on Christmas."

"There's nothing weird about early film!" her grandfather protested, already scrolling through the streaming service's app. "None of you have an appreciation for the art, so yes, fine, I will choose something pedestrian, solely for the enjoyment of others."

Jasmine followed her mother into the kitchen and closed the door behind them, aware that for some reason, she felt like she was being called into the principal's office. "So, where do we start?" she asked, opening the refrigerator. "What goes in first?"

"Turkey," her mother answered, already peeling potatoes. "Why was Leah sleeping on the floor this morning?"

"What?" Jasmine asked, still staring into the fridge. Making eye contact would be a huge mistake. "You saw us, she was in bed with me."

"The spare blankets from the linen closet were on the floor by the window," her mother said evenly. "Along with the rainbow pillow I made you last year."

Jasmine pulled out several trays of food, including the enormous lasagna her mother had assembled the day before, while she was out. "It was just in case we got cold," she lied, and as the words left her mouth she wondered why the walls were starting to close in around her. "Why would I make her sleep on the floor?"

"I don't know, Jazz, you tell me." Her mother lifted the foil on the uncooked lasagna, shoving it to the side. "Turkey first," she said sharply. Whatever battle they were fighting, Jasmine was losing.

"Does it really matter?" Jasmine asked, hefting the weight of the full-sized turkey from the shelf onto the island, sliding it across the pristine tiles. "Why do you even care?"

Her mother breathed out a long, quiet sigh. "I just want what's best for you, Jasmine. I don't want you to go through what I did."

"Dad left because he couldn't deal with any of it," Jasmine retorted. "Not Damien, and not me. Leah is my girlfriend, not my wife, so I don't know why this all has to be so serious right now."

"Do you want her to be your wife?" her mother asked. "Do you see a future with her?"

"Can we please just get through dinner first?" Jasmine shot back, punctuating her question with a sardonic laugh. "There's no marriage proposal, we've only been together three months, and you are pushing your luck right now."

Her mother glared at her as she separated the skin from the meat, pressing a compound butter of garlic and herbs into the gap she'd created. "I'm pushing my luck?" she demanded. "I'm trying to keep you safe."

"From Leah!" Jasmine shot back. "You're so preoccupied with Dad that you refuse to even try dating, and you spend all your time following me around, asking too many questions. I am twenty-eight years old, and I can manage my own personal life, thank you very much." She dropped a plastic container of peeled carrots onto the counter, sending one of them to catapult out onto the floor. "And it's not like Leah is a player, or a monster, or any of the other things you're so worried about. She's just a girl I work with, and I like her. Alright?"

"Hey, in here," her grandfather said, poking his head into the kitchen. "It sounds a little heated. We can hear you in the living room, Annie." He closed the door behind himself, bracing his hands against the back of one of the stools. "I thought we agreed not to argue this year?"

"Who's arguing, Dad?" Jasmine's mother washed her hands under the hot water, suds foaming away any trace of the food preparation. "We were just having a discussion about why the spare blankets were all on the floor in Jasmine's room this morning."

Before Jasmine could begin the argument anew, her grandfather laid a hand on her mother's arm. "Annie, enough," he said gently. "Not today."

She shook herself loose, shooting him a dirty look. "I don't need you scolding me, thank you very much." She crammed the turkey into the oven and slammed the door, the glass rattling against the hinges. "All I did was ask an honest question, and I was met with nothing but hostility."

"Because you never let up!" Jasmine interjected. "You don't trust me to make decisions, to live on my own, to choose who I do or don't date. I just need some space, alright?" She shook the carrots out onto a baking sheet, spreading them across the aluminum. "And Paps is right, you should download an app or something, get out of the house, go on dates." She risked a glance upwards at her mother, who didn't look as angry as she'd feared. "I know you worry, but I'm fine."

"And if you aren't fine tomorrow?" her mother asked quietly. "What then? Will Leah drive you to doctor's appointments? Across state lines to see a specialist? Will she cook you food that will nourish you?" She shook her head, taking the tray of carrots from her. "I know you think I am overbearing, I am only being cautious."

Jasmine fought the urge to cross her arms over her chest in a final act of defiance. "Not everyone is Dad."

"Plenty are," her mother argued.

"And plenty aren't!" Jasmine returned to the refrigerator, wresting the green bean casserole from her grandpa. "Will you please tell her to relax?"

Her mother tossed a metal spoon onto the counter. "I don't like that you two always gang up on me."

"Mom," Jasmine started, abandoning the crockery on the table to wrap her mother in an embrace, "I am asking you, please, to stop staring into the crystal ball of the future. I think what you're really angry about is that job I applied for."

Her mother shook her off, preparing the ham with cloves studded across its surface. "I'm not angry at all, Jazzy. I just want you to be happy."

"Then let's just have a nice Christmas, okay?" Jasmine offered, releasing her. "We can talk about how awful and terrifying everything is tomorrow after Leah leaves. I just... don't want you scaring her off, alright?"

"And I'm trying to make sure she isn't easily scared off," her mother countered. "If she can't handle a little bit of questioning, if you can't, then how will your relationship survive a hospitalization?"

"You can help her, Paps," Jasmine said, swallowing back plenty of snide words she would only regret. "I didn't bring Leah here for interrogation, I brought her because—" She stopped short, unsure of how much to share. "I brought her because she's never had a nice holiday, and I was under the clearly mistaken impression that the three of us could keep it together for three days. Obviously, I was wrong." She yanked open the kitchen door, already reaching for her parka. "Leah, do you want to go for a walk?"

"Sure," Leah replied from the other room, getting up off the sofa with the soft crunch of the upholstery. "Is it like a family tradition, or—" she stopped short when she saw the expression on Jasmine's face. "Everything okay?"

"Peachy." Jasmine pulled on her boots and wrested open the front door, only to discover a brown package sitting on the steps. "When did this get here?" she asked.

"I don't know, maybe it was a special delivery," her grandfather suggested, bending down to collect it. "It's from California." He handed it to Jasmine, and she tried hard to ignore the pleading expression on his face. "It's for you."

Jasmine took the box, turning it over in her hands. It was heavier than she'd expected, given the size. There was no name on the return address, but some part of her just knew where it had come from. "It's from Damien," she announced, closing the door.

"What is it?" her mother demanded, angrily folding and unfolding a dish towel in the doorway. "A request for your other kidney, maybe?"

"Annie," Jasmine's grandfather warned. "Not today, come on." He wrapped an arm around her shoulders, tugging her closer.

Leah held the box gingerly as Jasmine cut through the packing tape with the edge of her car key, sawing away at it. She really should have grabbed scissors from the kitchen, but the prospect of having to wait even thirty more seconds to see what was in the box was incomprehensible. One side, and then the other lifted free until she was able to pry the cardboard apart, revealing something encased in polystyrene and red tissue paper.

She lifted it out of the box, letting the packaging fall to the ground. "It's a snow globe," she said, emotion already thick in her throat. "It's from somewhere called Half Moon Bay." She shook it, holding it up to the light so they could all see the white glitter float, suspended in the water until it fell back to the base.

"There's a card," Leah said, nodding to the box that she was still holding. "There, in the bottom."

Jasmine tugged out the green envelope, not even properly sealed, just neatly folded in closure. The front had an image of a reindeer surfing a large wave, wearing comically oversized glasses. Flipping it open, she revealed an interior packed with cramped writing, along with a letter folded inside. She scanned the handwriting, catching every third phrase. *I'm sorry,* one read. *It's been too long,* said another. She folded it back up, sliding it into the envelope for safekeeping. "He wants to come visit after the new year," she said.

Her mother didn't say anything, but pressed her lips into a thin line.

"How is he?" her grandpa asked. "Doing well? Healthy?"

"Damien won a tournament," Jasmine said, the inevitable tears choking her with the lump in her throat. "He's doing really well, and... he's sorry he wasn't around more, you know, after."

Leah pulled her into an embrace, letting Jasmine hide her tears in the red buffalo check plaid, her sniffles muted by the brushed cotton. "That's good, right?" Leah asked gently.

"Mhm," Jasmine mumbled, nodding. "I'm just glad he's okay." She wrapped her arms around Leah's waist, kicking off her boots at the same time. All the fight she'd had just a few minutes prior had leaked out onto the floor, invisibly melting between the slats of the wood.

Chapter Twenty

"Alright, people, here we go," Martin announced proudly, arranging the final dish on the island. "Come take what you please, there's plenty of everything."

Jasmine poked Leah in the ribs. "Want me to go first?"

Leah nodded, following behind her as she filled her plate with a little of everything, including a fresh dinner roll straight from the oven, slathered in salted butter and perched atop the mashed potatoes because there was no more room for anything else. "This looks incredible, Annie," she offered, hoping to heal whatever rift there was, not that it would matter for very long. She'd leave in the morning, and that would be that.

"I hope it tastes as good as it looks," Annie replied, her intonation still a bit off, ever since the package had been discovered on the front step earlier. She patted Leah on the arm, her brow furrowed like she didn't know which end was up. "I'm sorry about earlier," she whispered as soon as Jasmine was back at the table. "My dad said you heard everything from the living room."

"Some," Leah lied. She'd heard every word. "I understand you're just worried." She took a second roll, spreading butter across the fluffy, steaming center. "If anyone gets hurt here, it won't be Jasmine." Once again, truth tumbled out of her mouth without permission, and she internally vowed to become a hermit in the woods once Christmas was all over. At least there, no one would hear her spewing such nonsense. She turned and mechanically walked back to the table, hoping that Annie would forget what she'd said.

Martin cleared his throat, fork in one hand, and knife in the other. "We don't really do the whole saying grace thing here, but I do want to say I am happy we are all here. Happy, healthy, and maybe by this time next year, a little bit wealthy."

"Amen," Jasmine answered with a giggle, pouring herself a glass of sparkling water. "Want some?" she offered.

Leah nodded, sipping from her champagne flute as soon as she'd finished. "Thank you for inviting me," she said again. "If I was at home, I'd probably be eating boxed mac and cheese on my own in front of the television." She sliced her meat into polite pieces, despite knowing she could devour them whole.

"A toast," Martin said, raising his glass of white wine. "To Leah, who has yet to run screaming from this house. And to Jasmine, who has been plotting this for months."

Leah and Jasmine exchanged a nervous glance, but raised theirs anyway in celebration. Annie joined them with her own, and added, "I'm starving, Dad. Enough with fake grace and toasts, there are only four of us. There's no need to posture. Save the speeches for the wedding." She nudged Jasmine's elbow, smirking.

"Mom, stop!" Jasmine said with a laugh, jabbing at her with a fork. "Hasn't Leah been through enough already?" She took a delicate bite, her eyes rolled to the ceiling. "These potatoes are next level," she praised. "Even better than last year."

"They'd better be, I spent an extra two dollars and forty-three cents for the better ones," Annie replied, arranging her plate into neat piles of sliced food, none of it touching. "But I'm glad you like it."

Every bite was like heaven. Leah struggled to pace herself, knowing that the others would notice if she wolfed down the entire plate like she wanted to. The full moon was only one more day away, and despite all the years of work she'd put into being able to better control her shifts, it was always easier with a full stomach. The turkey was juicy and seasoned, the ham spiced, the potatoes creamy with punches of garlic and rosemary, and the green bean casserole, which she'd left until last, was surprisingly tasty. The fried onions on top lent a nice crunch, and Leah found herself resisting the urge to go for seconds before the rest had even gotten through half their meal.

"Did you grow up with brothers?" Annie asked, gesturing at Leah's plate. "I've never known someone to eat so much so fast."

Leah nodded. "I did. And that whole fast metabolism thing means I get hungrier faster."

"Go, have more!" Martin urged, waving her back to the island with the casual gesture of his empty fork. "There's plenty!"

She hesitated, but only for a moment. The allure of a second helping was just too much to bear. Chair legs scraped against the floor as she stood and returned to the platters, taking more green beans this time, but also loading up on ham, potatoes, and two more dinner rolls loaded with butter.

"I don't know where she puts it," Jasmine mused, giving her a backward glance over her shoulder. "I'm barely halfway through and I know I won't be able to finish." She scraped together another bite, dragging the fork tines through the pool of gravy. "You know, of everything bad or annoying that happened this year, meeting Leah was the highlight."

Leah's cheeks flushed red, embarrassed by the compliment, even though it was an obvious lie.

"Who would have thought that working at Syndicorp would lead to something so nice?" Jasmine mused. She hadn't yet realized what she'd said, but Annie had. She put her fork down on the plate and glared over Jasmine's head at Leah.

"At Syndicorp?" she echoed.

"Leah usually works the floor, but I'm usually on cash," Jasmine explained, still unaware of her misstep. "But we manage to find time to chat, don't we, babe?"

"Jasmine," Leah said quietly.

Annie tapped her butter knife against the edge of the porcelain. "You met Leah at Syndicorp, where you've only been working for three weeks?" she pressed. "So I can only assume that you lied to us about some aspect of this, so which is it? You two have only just started dating, what, five minutes ago? Or are you even dating at all?"

Jasmine cleared her throat, fork still halfway to her mouth before she abandoned it. "I, uh—"

"Is she even your girlfriend, Jazz?" Annie demanded. "Have you been lying to us this entire time? For what?" She stood up and pointed at Leah. "And you! What kind of person lies to their host for free food?"

Leah shook her head vehemently, stepping back from the island. "No, Annie, that's not—"

"Dad?" Annie prompted. "Did you know about this?"

Martin swallowed, tapping his calloused fingers against the green cotton tablecloth, the center of it creased from spending all year in storage. "No," he said finally. "I didn't. Though, I suppose, it clears up a few things, like why Jasmine didn't know Leah was a geologist, or why Leah hadn't heard about Damien." He stayed seated, but his face was one of being profoundly wounded. It sliced through to Leah's core.

She wanted to reach out for Jasmine, to exact some form of reassurance, or to wake up from whatever nightmare she'd found herself in, but there was no rest for the wicked, no respite for liars and con artists. "I should go," she said finally.

No one protested.

Not even Jasmine.

***

Leah awoke to her cell phone buzzing against her nightstand the next morning, rattling angrily against the lamp. It was work, and she had seventeen missed calls.

"Hello?" she grumbled into the speaker, the covers still pulled up over her head. Whatever their emergency was, it was categorically not her problem.

"Where are you, Ms. Erickson?"

"I, uh—Mrs. Campbell?" Leah asked. "I'm—" she couldn't remember what excuse she'd used on the rejected time off request. "I'm not at home," she lied.

"Then you'd better be on your way to work," Mrs. Campbell barked. "You are already ninety minutes late for your shift. I warned you about this last week, you can't just—"

"It's not my shift anymore," Leah explained. "Jasmine Reed, the girl you told me to ask, took the shift. It's on the swaps board."

"Ms. Reed never showed up, didn't call in, and hasn't answered my calls," Mrs. Campbell replied, acid dripping from every syllable. "And as such, the shift is still yours to work. The entire shop floor is looking like a disaster area. You have fifteen minutes to get here, Ms. Erickson, or you will be filing for unemployment tomorrow morning."

"She didn't answer?" Leah asked, bolting up in bed. "Did you try her cell? Her house?"

"Yes, obviously, but no one answered. Fifteen minutes, Ms. Erickson."

The line went dead, and as it did, Leah was already halfway out of her single bed, tugging on the previous day's jeans. She dialed Jasmine, but it went straight to voicemail three times. Something was wrong. No matter what had happened on Christmas, Jasmine wouldn't leave Leah to get fired. That wasn't who she was.

It was only noon, but the sky was darkened with grey clouds already. The shift rippled under Leah's skin, a promise of what would come later. Checking the silver hoops in her ears, she dialed Jasmine's number again.

It went straight to voicemail without even one single ring. Leah didn't have the house number, if there even was one, nor did she have a way to contact Annie or Martin. She threw open the curtains, surprised at the icy draft already seeping beneath the windowsill, enough to make even Leah shiver.

She pulled on a thick hoodie, shoving her feet into winter boots. She only had a few hours to make sure Jasmine was safe before the shift would come, and she had to be out by the forest by then or risk discovery. Her keys were heavy in her hands, the weight of Annie's words too loud in her ears about Jasmine's medical history. What if she had passed out at the wheel? What if she was already in the hospital? Leah considered calling, but it wasn't like the receptionists would tell her anything. She was no one to Jasmine, nothing more than a coworker.

And yet, Leah didn't think twice about abandoning her job to look for her.

Chapter Twenty-One

Jasmine shivered, pulling her arms tight around herself to try for warmth, but found none. She'd always had trouble keeping warm after her long stints in the hospital, the air always too crisp to be comfortable unless she was lying in the sun.

She mourned its absence, the skies dark and swirling with clouds that were probably laden with snow. The car's display remained inert, with no gauge for temperature or anything else. The battery had given up the ghost two hours back, after spending too long with her hazards on, willing someone to pass by.

Mud, ice, and slush had flooded the road, careening down the tree farm's steep slope, dug out for the road, and slamming into the driver's side door, pinning her car against the opposing cliff face. She was trapped, and despite bargains with the universe, and praying to good fortune, the wheels spun in the mud, the car unmoving.

Checking her watch for the nine-hundred-and-forty-seventh time, Jasmine's stomach churned. It would only be another hour until sunset, if that. The sun, whatever small amount there was, had already dipped below the horizon, and it wasn't strong enough to paint a final sunset along the flat landscape.

Her phone had been dead since she left the house that morning, rushing to work to cover Leah's shift. The previous night had been so fraught with arguments and strife that she hadn't checked to make sure it was charging. It hadn't, and so she was stranded, left adrift, and no one knew where she was.

Her mother and grandpa didn't even know she was missing—as far as they knew, she wasn't due home for another two hours. They'd wait another hour after that before they tried to call her first, and then the store, and only then would they start to panic. Even so, she'd taken the scenic route to town, craving the quiet contemplation of the countryside to clear her troubled mind. Except she'd had several frozen hours of contemplation at that point, and there was nothing she wanted more than a hot drink, several blankets, and Leah.

Jasmine breathed into her hands, rubbing them together. It didn't help much. Her toes had been numb for a long while already, and with the sun slipping down over the road in the distance, the temperature was dropping rapidly. She was no expert in first aid, but she knew enough to realize that unless she was found, she might not last the night. Even if she was found, hypothermia could damage her one remaining kidney. It was a common affliction, easily healed for most, but for her, it could set off another chain reaction that would send her back to the hospital for months.

"I'm sorry, Leah," she said aloud, swallowing back a sob. Jasmine never should have let her leave. Should have chased her down the sidewalk and begged her to stay, or left with her, or anything other than remaining at the dinner table to spend three hours arguing with her mother. It was the same as it always was, nothing new, always the central theme of how Jasmine couldn't take care of herself.

She huffed out a sardonic laugh, amused at her own blockheadedness. "I guess you were right, Mom," she muttered. "Look where I wound up."

Jasmine tried again to shove open the driver's side door. If she could escape the car, she could at least try to walk the last five miles. Wind swirled around the car, bringing with it the delicate dance of relocated snowflakes, scraped from the nearby drift. If the cold didn't kill her, the wind might.

She shoved with all her might, even using her legs to push out against the door, but it was locked in place by the solidifying mass of mud and ice that was high enough that she couldn't even see through the window. Jasmine had already tried to kick out the glass to no avail. Her legs were too shaky, a combination of cold and low blood sugar that she couldn't escape.

Her watch ticked another minute forward, and then another. She'd been so sure when her car got pinned by the landslide that someone would be along in a few minutes and stop to help, or at least to call someone. And yet, somehow, no one had come. It was the day after Christmas, most people were at home hiding from the cold, and the sparsely populated area around the road didn't help. Where it was lively a week back, it was quiet, a narrow, ghostly highway around the tree farm.

The last remnants of light vanished, leaving her in hopeless darkness. She breathed, and the sound of quiet exhalations was enough to dominate the soundscape. She was so tired. Maybe, if she just slept a while, someone would come along. Someone would find her. They had to. A landslide couldn't be how she went out. Her mother would be devastated. Her grandpa would never be the same, and Leah—Jasmine shook her head. Leah was long gone.

She thought she saw headlights on the horizon, and for a split second her heart surged with hope in her chest until she realized they were nothing more than distant street lights flicking on. There weren't any on the stretch of road she was trapped on. Budget cuts, they'd said. Not enough people traveling along that road to merit paying for a few light bulbs, a few hours a night. According to them, it was a waste of city resources.

Jasmine slunk down in her seat, waiting for death, waiting for sleep, waiting for rescue, whatever came first. Whichever took her first, she would accept it, because she didn't have any energy left to fight. It had all gone to keep her warm, and on trying to dislodge any of the doors to escape. Futility's despair sank deep into her bones, its tendrils racing past even the frozen whispers caressing her skin.

The sky grew darker, and then faded into a wintery blue, the depths of which were both incomprehensible and claustrophobic. She'd never been afraid of small spaces before. It had always been the wide-open, indiscriminate future that kept her up at night with its promises and its lies. She'd been so close to something new, but all it had led to was backsliding, a hopeless return to where she'd been for years. A decade wasn't much, but at the same time, it was fundamental to her personhood and inescapable.

Something moved in the trees across the lanes, a huge, shadowy figure lurking within the safety of foliage. Jasmine watched, unconcerned. It was a hallucination, something her subconscious played out as a movie to frighten her into action, but there was nothing left to be done but wait.

The shadow paced between the tall firs and the empty stumps at the top of the embankment, some of them already torn out to ready the space for replanting. It seemed like it was looking for something, or choosing between two paths. Perhaps it was symbolic. Or, and more likely, it was her swan song before she slipped into a quiet rest she'd never wake up from. It wasn't a bad way to go. There were far worse ways to die.

"Hello," Jasmine said, waving to the figment. Cheap entertainment, playing with her own mind, but it was better than the nothingness she'd been enduring for hours. "Fancy meeting you here."

The figure paused and seemed to be staring straight at her. It emerged from the trees a huge, hulking grizzly bear, lumbering across the displaced earth with enormous paws capped with long claws that could shred her in an instant.

"Oh, heck," Jasmine said, shoving herself into the passenger side seat. If that bear was a hallucination, it was certainly one of the most convincing. Not even anesthesia caused visions like that, and she never took to sedatives all that well.

If the cold didn't get her, the bear might. It approached slowly, walking around the more dangerous portions of the mudslide. Did bears know navigation? She supposed they must, if they returned to the same places year after year. But then, bears shouldn't be in the Midwest. They were far too south for bears, especially one that size, and particularly in late December, which should have been peak hibernation season for a grizzly.

The bear moved closer to the car, still cloaked in darkness, but its black eyes flashed a glare from those distant street lights as it considered whether or not to eat Jasmine from the head down, or the feet up. It circled the car from about six feet out, as much as it could with it pinned against the retaining wall, the chicken wire to keep rocks from the road mangled and torn.

Jasmine's breath grew shallow in her lungs, the fear sinking its teeth into her without hesitation. Adrenaline, at least, was one way to find the energy to look for some sort of weapon to fend it off with. She hadn't been able to break through the glass, but that bear might, being several hundred pounds heavier. There was a heavy-duty ice scraper in the back seat, one side with a sharp, resin edge, and the other a soft, useless snow brush.

She held it aloft as the bear pawed at the mud beneath her tires, the quiet scraping more of an immediate threat than the encroaching cold. Jasmine smacked the window. "Go away!" she shouted, brandishing the ice scraper. "Get out of here!"

The bear looked at her just for a moment before returning to pawing at the mud. It wasn't threatened by Jasmine's threats, and less so by her theatrics.

Jasmine banged on the window again, screaming. "Go!" she yelled. "Leave me alone!" She waved her arms around, despite knowing that the bear would likely not even see her with all the mud and snow pressed against the window and the part of the windshield. "Someone is going to hit you with their car!" she pleaded. "Also I don't want to be eaten! I'm too stringy!"

The bear dug further, allowing one tire to reconnect with the road. It wasn't enough to free her, but it was a start, so long as the beast didn't remember how hungry it was. Jasmine couldn't imagine there was much food to be had out there. Maybe the bear was starving. Worse, maybe it was rabid. It would explain its strange gait and its presence in the middle of winter.

Jasmine pressed her hand against the window, half-frozen tears leaking from her eyes. "Please," she said. "I don't want to go yet. I know you don't, either, but if you let me live I swear I'll make sure you do, too."

The bear stopped pawing at the mud and sat back on its haunches, staring. Whether it was a hungry stare or a confused one, Jasmine couldn't tell. It made a strange sound in its throat, a horrifying, guttural noise that sounded like the threat of a painful death.

"I promise!" Jasmine screamed. "Please, just leave me alone!" She pushed herself back into the passenger seat as far as she could go, as if that would save her if the bear wanted to break through the window and eat her as a tasty snack. It returned to the mud, scraping it away one chunk at a time. The front driver's side lurched forward as the tire was freed, rubber meeting tarmac with the soft whump of impact.

She stayed as still as she could, squinting through the fogged windows as the bear moved to the back of the car, scratching at the earth holding her car in place. It was strange behavior for a bear, but maybe it had escaped from a zoo. Or, she'd been right about it being rabid, and it was about sixty seconds from feasting on her limbs like a turkey leg at the county fair.

The back of the car wobbled, rocking back and forth as the bear put its weight on the bumper, moving side to side as the tires sank further into the mud. She'd been hopeful, maybe, for a time, but the last glimmer fizzled when the bear smacked the back window, leaning over the trunk of the car to stare inside, squinting through the condensation that had collected over hours of Jasmine breathing, trying to keep warm.

The moon crested up over the horizon, the white-blue glow casting a ghostly hue over the abandoned stretch of road. If ever there was a moment for a car to pass by, that was it, and yet the reflectors implanted into the ground remained inert, echoing only the light of the moon.

In years of hospital visits, of doctors telling her that she might not make it, that she'd never be the same, she never felt any kind of palpable fear, because she'd made her decision with the full knowledge of what could happen. She didn't regret it, and never had, not even for a second. Yet, in that moment, regrets flashed across her mind's eye like a terrible movie, revisiting every harsh word she'd ever spoken, every failure to establish a real career, and her biggest and most recent shame: letting Leah go.

A sob caught in Jasmine's throat as she pushed herself further down into the seat, half of her squeezed between the dashboard and the torn upholstery. "Please," she whispered. "Please, please."

The bear made another strange sound as the back left wheel was released from the mud, a kind of throaty shout. Through the misty window, it stared at Jasmine, something glinting in its ear.

Jasmine leaned forward, trying to make it out. A tag, probably, and most likely from a zoo or a sanctuary, but the nearest one was at least an hour's drive, and there had been nothing in the news about a huge, escaped grizzly. At least if it was from an enclosure, it was unlikely to be rabid, at least, she hoped that was the case. She fell asleep in her zoology class more than once in college, and she'd skipped it at least three times to study for other exams.

But it wasn't a tag at all. There were three silver hoops through the bear's ear, just like Leah's.

Jasmine stared, and shook her head. The cold was getting to her. She was hallucinating, but it was difficult to know whether she was imagining the earrings, or the bear entirely.

"No," she said evenly. "That can't be. I'm losing it."

The bear freed the back right tire, scraping mud from beneath the bumper and flinging it behind the car, chunks raining down in the night air and splattering onto the pavement. Only one was left trapped by the mudslide, the one directly beneath Jasmine. She scrambled back into the driver's seat, trying to start the car, but with the battery dead, it wouldn't even try to turn over.

The bear stopped at the front of the car, ears pricked up as it listened to the sad ticking, and the lack of engine noise springing to life.

"It's dead," Jasmine explained, a little unsure why she was talking to a bear like that. It wasn't like it could understand her. "And I can't get out of the car and walk, because you will eat me, and it's too cold."

It tilted its head and just like that, wandered back into the woods.

She didn't have long to weigh the risks of walking the five miles to town in the freezing cold, because ten minutes after the bear vanished, a tow truck and an ambulance arrived to whisk her away.

Chapter Twenty-Two

Leah paced the corridor of the intensive care unit, hoping for a clue as to which room Jasmine was in. The front desk wouldn't tell her, not being family, but the idea that Jasmine was alone and suffering the effects of hypothermia wasn't one she could easily bear.

She pulled at the earrings in her cartilage, grateful at least that something gave her the clarity to help, to spend the afternoon and evening driving every road looking for Jasmine, tracking and backtracking until the shift was inevitable.

"Leah?" Annie asked, exiting the elevator, her face a mixture of terror and anger. "What the hell are you doing here?"

"I, uh—" Leah started.

"She's in room thirty-four," Martin supplied, ignoring the sharp jab to his ribs from his daughter. "We just asked at reception." He tilted his head, his eyes narrowed. "How did you know she was here? The hospital only just called us an hour ago and we rushed right over. Had to warm up the car first, though, the batteries hate this weather."

"Uh, work," Leah answered. It was at least partly true. "She missed a shift and they called me to take it. I couldn't get hold of her, I worried, and..." she trailed off because her story wasn't making sense. "Work," she repeated.

Annie stormed past her, marching up the tiled corridor matching the room number. "They shouldn't be giving you that information," she snarled. "And neither should the hospital be telling them that Jasmine is sick. It's a legal violation of HIPAA."

"I just wanted to make sure she's okay," Leah said, following her down the hallway with matching squeaks of damp boot treads against waxed floors. "And I'm sorry, you know, about Christmas, I—"

Annie whirled around, pointing at her just outside Jasmine's room. "I don't want to hear it. You lied to us in our own home, and for what? Because you wanted a free meal?"

"No, it's more complicated than that, she—"

"Leah?" Jasmine called softly from the other side of the door. "Is that you?"

Martin eased it open, the hinges well-oiled and silent. He opened his arms, gesturing for Leah to go in.

"Dad, I don't think—" Annie started.

"Annie, she's asking for Leah," he replied firmly. "If she's conscious, she's stable."

Leah edged past Annie, her skin almost searing off under the heat of her angry stare. "Hey," she said brightly, giving Jasmine a half-hearted wave. "I just wanted to make sure you were okay." She stood at the foot of the bed, cramming her hands into her pockets. "Are you?"

"What time is it?" Jasmine asked, nodding at the clock on the wall. "It's busted."

"Seven," Leah answered.

Jasmine squinted at her, tugging the thick blankets up over herself and tucking in the edges. "I'm happy to see you, but how did you know I was here?"

"Work," Leah replied, aware that Annie and Martin were right behind her. Even if they weren't there, she'd have kept the same story anyway, hoping that Jasmine didn't dig any further.

"Work," Jasmine repeated. "Yeah, of course. Mrs. Campbell never knows when to keep her mouth shut, does she?"

"No, she doesn't," Annie said, taking the opportunity to barge into the room with the large duffel bag she'd been carrying on her arm. "I brought you clean clothes and toiletries, Jazz, as well as that conditioner you like."

"They're letting me out in a few hours," Jasmine replied. "I'm only in this ward because it was a free bed. They gave me fluids, they warmed me up, they're just checking blood work and I'll be able to go home."

Annie's lips pressed into a thin line as she dropped the bag on the horrible plasticky chair in the corner. "I don't think we should make any assumptions. We should prepare for this to be a longer stay. I'll call your boss, and after I tear her a new one, I'll inform them that you'll be needing an extended leave of absence."

"I'm fine, Mom," Jasmine said firmly. "I feel fine. Look, I even ate the terrible breakfast they brought." She gestured towards the empty tray on the side table, nothing left except cold toast crumbs and a streak of butter smeared across one side. "In fact, I could eat more."

"Let's go fish up something in the cafeteria," Martin suggested, pulling gently on Annie's arm. "I've been missing that lime jello, and I bet Jazzy wouldn't mind some bacon, right?"

Jasmine nodded, pushing herself into a sitting position and adjusting the bed to match her posture. "Sounds great, Paps."

Annie chewed her lip, wanting to argue, but followed Martin out into the hallway anyway, shooting daggers at Leah as she went.

"So," Jasmine said, patting the bit of empty bed next to her. "I think we need to talk."

Leah sat, smoothing wrinkles from the rest of the bedspread. "About Christmas?" she asked. "I'm sorry, I shouldn't have left."

"I don't blame you," Jasmine replied, pulling her hair into a messy bun at the top of her head, twisting the hair tie around until it had secured her long, thick locks. "But that's not what I meant."

"No?" Leah asked, panic rising in her like high tide, and the undertow just as deadly.

Jasmine tilted her head, folding her hands in her lap on top of the blankets. "No," she confirmed. "Leah, something weird happened last night."

"Oh?"

"This is going to sound unhinged, so I need you to promise me you won't tell my mom. She'll want to keep me in here for months." Jasmine drew in a deep breath, squeezing her eyes closed, her dark eyelashes scrunched together. "I was driving to work yesterday, you know, for your shift cover. I took the back roads because my mom and I spent the rest of Christmas arguing about our little charade."

Leah sucked her teeth, guilt surging from her feet directly into her throat, constricting her ability to breathe. "I'm sorry," she said. "I should have stayed."

"I was driving past the tree farm out on the highway," Jasmine explained. "There was a small mudslide, it came out of nowhere and pinned my car to the retaining wall."

"Oh no!" Leah said with a gasp, hoping her performance was believable, but it rarely was around pretty women. "Is that why you're here? Did you get crushed?"

"Those are nice earrings," Jasmine said. "Are they silver?"

"Uh..." Leah trailed off, almost choking on the fear that had hold of her tongue. "They are," she answered. "What happened to your car?"

"Towed to the local mechanic in town. The damage is mostly superficial, but it needs a new battery. I should be able to pick it up tomorrow." Jasmine reached out and took Leah's hand, rubbing her thumb over Leah's scraped knuckles. "How did this happen?"

"It's nothing," Leah said. "I was clearing out the garage."

"I was stuck out there for hours. The tow truck driver said the road had already been blocked off at the other end because there was another mudslide about a mile and a half up the road from where I got stuck. Looks like that guy at the farm was right." Jasmine drew in a breath, holding Leah's hand tighter. "A bear freed my car, but it wouldn't start."

"A bear," Leah repeated, putting on a surprised laugh. "There aren't any bears here."

"I thought I had imagined it, but after they loaded me into the ambulance, I heard two of the paramedics commenting on the weird footprints in the slush. I had to lie and say I didn't see anything."

Leah was all but backed into a corner. Jasmine had an idea, at least, and given half a chance it would bloom into certainty. "Surprise," Leah said softly. "I'm sorry, I know you don't like big surprises."

"Surprise, what?" Jasmine asked, apparently needing confirmation that Leah didn't want to give. "What did you do, Leah? Because ten minutes after that bear wandered back into the woods, I was rescued."

"I don't know what you want me to say." The words passed Leah's lips as a whisper, a waver in her voice that she couldn't steady. "I'm glad that you're alright, bear or no bear."

"Leah." Jasmine gripped her hand harder, pulling her closer. "I need you to tell me what happened, because otherwise I'm going to think I'm starting to lose it."

"It was cold," Leah explained, unable to meet her penetrating stare because if she did, then the game would be over. Jasmine would know, or at least think that Leah was admitting to something impossible. "And you were probably hungry? It's not beyond the scope that you'd see something that wasn't there."

"The paramedics, Leah. They saw the tracks, saw them leading back into the woods on the embankment. Something was out there." Jasmine clasped her other hand around Leah's, enclosing her fingers around Leah's wrist. "Was it you?" she breathed.

Leah summoned the last vestiges of courage from the base of her spine, drawing it up through each vertebra until she found the ability to answer. "What if I said yes?"

"Then I would have to thank you," Jasmine answered, her voice still low and soft. "Because I might have died, otherwise."

"You're stronger than you think," Leah offered. "And much stronger than your mother thinks." She inched closer to Jasmine, her heart pounding in her chest. "I'm just sorry it took me so long," she whispered.

"So it *was* you?" Jasmine confirmed, her brown eyes round as saucers, stunned and in awe. "I don't get it."

Leah shrugged. "Neither do I. There aren't many of us, but we're around." She let Jasmine drag her hands closer to the top of the blanket. "Campbell called me in the morning. I knew you wouldn't skip the shift, so I worried something was wrong. I drove around all day, until... well. You know."

"Full moon," Jasmine supplied. "You can't resist changing when that happens?”

"Not without a lot of pain." Leah shifted on the bed, the mattress squeaking beneath her weight. "During the day it feels like a bad hangover."

Jasmine pulled her hands free, nudging a cup of water towards Leah. "Here," she offered. "Drink this."

"No, that's yours," Leah said, holding her hands up in refusal. "I'll be fine, this happens every month."

"How do you keep from getting caught?" Jasmine breathed. "Is it still... *you*, in there?"

Leah pulled at her earrings, showing them off with a glint of light reflected against the whitewashed wall. "These help. They're silver, so when I am... well, when I'm that, it's enough discomfort to keep me a little more present in my body. I'm more able than most to be myself during those days, but it takes a toll in other ways."

"What kind of other ways?" Jasmine asked, taking a sip of water herself.

The straw gurgled in the empty cup, and Leah swallowed hard, wondering when the brutal honesty would stop and let her rest. "I'm lonely," she said finally. "It's hard to keep something like this a secret. People can usually tell that I'm hiding something, they just assume it's something like cheating, or fraud, or whatever." Leah shrugged, trying to laugh it off. "You sensed I was hiding something, too."

Jasmine nodded, picking at the lint on the top blanket. "For the record, I didn't think it was cheating or fraud."

"Oh?" Leah prompted. "And what did you think it was?"

"I thought you were competing for that job with me," Jasmine admitted. "You got so upset after I mentioned it, and it could potentially be a cross-disciplinary position, so I thought it must be that." She shrugged, the hospital gown baggy over her shoulders, draping down over her slender biceps. "I guess I was wrong."

"Oh," Leah repeated. "No, it wasn't that."

"There are two positions, you know," Jasmine suggested. She sighed quietly, gazing wistfully out the window over the overcast morning, tucking a stray, escaped hair back into place. "Archival, which is what I jumped for, of course. But there's also a research fellowship at the same park downstate, something to do with work around dating marine sedimentary rocks. I didn't mention it before, because you never told me you got your master's in geology." Jasmine poked her in the arm, an eyebrow raised in jest. "I think you should apply, unless Syndicorp has your heart."

Leah rubbed the thighs of her jeans, more an unconscious habit than a real bid for extra warmth. The hospital already verged on being too hot for her to be comfortable. "I think Syndicorp is in my past," she admitted. "Campbell told me she'd fire me unless I went in yesterday."

"And you didn't?" Jasmine asked.

"No," Leah replied, shaking her head. "I went looking for you, instead." She chewed voraciously on her lip, the dramatically oscillating emotions taking their toll. "I don't have a single regret."

"Will you come to New Year's?" Jasmine asked suddenly. "I will go home today, no matter what my mother says, but I still won't be up for any parties or anything." She leaned in close, pushing herself further down the bed until her lips were next to Leah's ear, breath ghosting across her neck and drawing goosebumps wherever it met. "And I'll need someone to kiss at midnight."

"I, uh—" Leah stammered, her thoughts racing in her head, crashing into one another with such force that she forgot whatever it was she was about to say.

"We're back!" Martin shouted from the hallway, nudging open the door with the toe of his boot. He was carrying a tray piled high with food, the tower of fruit cups ready to tumble to the floor. Leah took the items that wobbled the most, redistributing them to the wheeled table designed to slide over the hospital bed. "Thank you, Leah," he said. "You can have a fruit cup and a croissant as a reward." He caught her eye and offered up an encouraging smile. "You must be hungry."

"Mom, Leah is the one who found me," Jasmine announced. "My car got stuck on the highway behind the tree farm, the mudslide pinned me in. She came looking for me and dug me out."

Annie's glare swapped from one to the other, softening each time until a soft cry caught in her throat. "Why didn't you say so?" she asked, reaching out to pull Leah into a tight embrace. "How did you know where to find her?"

"I told you, I know that area," Leah replied, returning the embrace, albeit not as tightly. "And I didn't have either of your numbers to tell you. The store wouldn't give them to me." That last part was a lie, but a small one, necessary in order to hide her Bear self. "I'm sorry, I would have if I could have."

"But why?" Annie asked, still gripping the elbows of Leah's jacket with enough force to crumple the leather in her fingers. "I thought it was all a lie. Why risk being out in that cold? Why bother?"

Leah searched for words that wouldn't come. She tried to form some sort of sentence, to lie, to invent something else as a reason, to lie and say it was an accident that she'd even found Jasmine in the first place, but she couldn't. There had been enough lies in her past to last a lifetime. "It started that way," she explained. "As a lie. But..." she stumbled over her thoughts, failing to organize them in a poetic or at least realistic way. "I don't know, somewhere along the way, things changed."

A doctor entered, clipboard braced against her dark skin. "Hello, Ms. Reed," she said, looking around at the other three present. "Your results are in, do you want privacy?"

"Is it bad, Dr. Ahara?" Jasmine asked, her voice confident, prepared even for the worst.

"No, it's not bad," Dr. Ahara replied kindly. "Shall I proceed?" She waited for Jasmine to nod, and then began to read off the clipboard, running down the side with a blue pen. "Everything looks good. No damage to your existing kidney, in fact, your levels are better than some people who have both."

Annie crumpled into the chair, dropping the duffel to the floor. "No damage?" she asked quietly.

"No damage," Dr. Ahara confirmed. "I don't know if that would have been the case if you hadn't been brought in when you were. I'd recommend plenty of fluids and rest until you feel more put together, and then going for some walks would be good. You should be good as new in a week or two, Ms. Reed." The doctor flipped pages back on the clipboard, smiling down at Jasmine. "You've come a long way. However, I would gently suggest carrying a spare charger in your car."

Jasmine laughed softly, burying her face in her hands. "I know, I know," she groaned. "Never again."

Dr. Ahara checked the IV bag leading down into Jasmine's arm, nodding. "A nurse will be by in about an hour to get you ready for discharge if that sounds good to you."

"No offense, Dr. Ahara," Jasmine said, miming a whisper, "as much as people rave about the food here, my mom has some incredible leftovers that I can't wait to devour."

"Good, good," Dr. Ahara said with a laugh. "An appetite is good. I see your grandfather is already on that mission here, it looks like he sold the cafeteria out of everything halfway decent." She winked at Martin, a hand on her hip. "If I have to eat a sad, wilted salad for lunch, there will be hell to pay."

"Dr. Ahara, you've saved our Jazzy so many times, I'd hand deliver you a filet mignon if you asked for it." Martin offered her a fruit cup, but she declined.

"I'll remember that, I might just call it in." Dr. Ahara nodded at them all. "Have a good rest of the holiday season," she said. "Jasmine, I hope I don't see you again."

Chapter Twenty-Three

Jasmine paced the hallway, stopping each time she passed the mirror to check her hair, and then her makeup, her dress, obsessing over every detail.

"You look lovely," her grandpa said, resting his hands on her shoulders. "When is Leah getting here?"

"Any minute." Jasmine hugged him and then nudged him away to fix her hem, picking at a frayed thread emerging from one of the silvery sequins. "I don't know why I'm so nervous."

He grinned at her in their reflection and straightened his tie. "That's always the case when it's someone special. I felt the same way with your grandmother, our first date after Woodstock. We'd spent an amazing weekend together—"

"Ew, Paps, I don't need details," Jasmine interrupted.

"—And the next time I saw her, two weeks later, I was a wreck. Tripped up the porch steps and put my face through their screen door. Her father looked like he wanted to run me over with his car." He fussed with his tie again, pinning it with a moonstone tie tack that matched his cufflinks. "I won him over in the end when I fixed his television."

Boots crunched against freshly fallen snow up the walk, and Jasmine yanked open the door before Leah could even knock. "Hi," she said, noting the bouquet of daisies in her hand.

"Uh, hi," Leah replied. "These are for you." She handed over the flowers, the cellophane crinkling and sparkling in the glow from the foyer's overhead light. "I have to say, I feel a little under-dressed."

"It's just for fun," Jasmine said, pulling her inside and taking her coat, revealing a starched grey plaid shirt bedecked with a silvery tie, the contrast stark and sharp against her black jeans. "Besides, you look great."

"Martin, nice to see you again," Leah said, putting out her hand to shake his. "You look very smart tonight."

"I'm going out," he announced, turning towards the coat closet and blocking Jasmine from sliding the door closed. "There's a swing dance night at the community center tonight. Free shuttle." He did a strange, stilted two-step on the wood floor.

Jasmine lifted an eyebrow. "Since when are you into swing dancing?"

"I'm still young, Jazzy, I'm allowed to develop new interests." He shrugged on a black blazer, buttoning it before he topped it with a thick parka. "And my friend Mel said it's a great place to meet women." He wiggled his eyebrows and kissed her on the forehead. "Have fun tonight. I'm sorry I can't stay! Tell your mom—"

"Tell your mom what?" her mother interjected. "Where are you off to, Dad?"

"Swing dancing, apparently," Jasmine supplied. "You look nice. Seems like a waste you're all cuted up just to spend New Year's with us."

Her mother twirled on the spot, the skirt of her dress fanning out as she spun. "I'm not. I have a date." She reached into the closet and took out her coat, slipping on a pair of heels with an ankle strap. "Jazz, can I borrow these?"

"As long as you promise you won't break anything," Jasmine replied. She'd anticipated an evening of friendly conversation, and that Leah would drive home in the early morning, but the prospect of having the house to themselves was almost more than she could bear. "Call me if you need anything, we'll just be here."

Her mother hugged her, and she smelled of lavender, a perfume she hadn't worn in years. "Don't wait up, okay?"

"Yeah," her grandpa echoed. "Don't wait up."

"Well, everyone has plans but us," Jasmine said, slipping an arm around Leah's waist, feeling her abs tense at the light pressure and suddenly, Jasmine couldn't get them out of the house fast enough. "I can't promise there will be leftovers after we raid the fridge."

"Raid away," her mother said, halfway out the door. "I hid all the good stuff anyway."

"It's under the soup tureen," Jasmine's grandpa said, following her out into the dark, cold night. "In the green bowl, the one with the chickens on it."

Leah mimed taking notes on her phone, nodding sagely. "I've preserved that for the archives," she said, nudging Jasmine back. "Seeing as the resident archivist didn't do it yet."

"It's just an interview!" Jasmine protested, laughing. "I don't want to get too excited yet. Let me make sure I don't bomb it first." She waved off her mother and grandpa, deadbolting the door once they climbed into their respective transport, her grandpa into a shuttle, and her mother into her date's car. "So," she said, turning back to Leah. "It looks like we have the place to ourselves."

Leah's hazel eyes flashed with intensity, but she bit her lip. "Do you want to watch a movie or something?"

"Sure," Jasmine said, padding into the next room with nothing on her feet except the thin nylon of her black tights. She tugged at the hem of her dress as she knelt down in front of the movie cabinet, sifting through titles until she found the one she'd been looking for. "I bought a copy," she said, showing it off. "I wanted us to watch it together, your bad horror movie. It's not Christmas anymore."

"I don't know if horror is the best way to start a new year, either," Leah replied, leaning casually against the door frame. "So I guess we better finish it before midnight." Her eyes dragged across Jasmine's frame, nodding appreciatively. "You look phenomenal."

"What, this old thing?" Jasmine asked, straightening. "I've had it for years."

"The tag is still on the back." Leah smirked, disappearing into the kitchen. "Drink?" she called over the sound of bottles clinking. "Sparkling?"

"Sure," Jasmine replied, willing her face to stop flushing. She ripped the tag off, cursing at it under her breath. She shoved it under a couch cushion, knowing she'd forget about it. "Thanks," she said, taking the fluted glass of sparkling water.

Leah sat next to her on the sofa, their thighs touching as the opening credits played over a cheesy soundtrack from the eighties, all synth pads and repetitive drum machine measures. "I applied for that job," she said, sipping from her glass.

"Oh?" Jasmine prompted, setting her own on the coffee table. "And?"

"I got the email yesterday, they want to interview me next week. In person, downstate." Leah ruffled her freshly cropped hair, even shorter than it had been before, and it suited her, showing off her sharp cheekbones and wide, beautiful eyes. "I thought maybe we could drive down together, make a weekend of it."

"Oh, yes," Jasmine replied eagerly. "I was envisioning having to ride with my mom and grandpa, they'd be making me do interview preparation all the way down there." She laid a hand on Leah's knee, and the proximity was already clouding her conscious thoughts. "I'm glad you got an interview."

"I don't want to get too excited yet," Leah warned, but laid a hand on top of Jasmine's. "Just in case it doesn't work out."

"You don't like excitement?" Jasmine asked, hiking up her dress so that she could straddle Leah on the couch. She'd waited long enough, damn it. She pressed her hands to either side of Leah's neck and leaned in until their lips met.

A tiny, repressed moan escaped Leah's throat, and she grabbed Jasmine's hips, pulling her closer, and then sliding down to run her hands up her thighs, toying with the sequined hemline as she inched further. "How are you feeling?" she asked, pulling back for a second.

"Shut up," Jasmine said, kissing her again, this time opening her mouth to deepen their connection, their tongues sliding against each other delicately, just enough to act as a further temptation for later. It started as a demure tightening between her thighs, but quickly grew into her rotating her hips against Leah, already craving so much more than that.

Leah responded in kind, wrapping her hands around Jasmine's thighs, inching ever closer to the inside, her fingertips gentle but needy through the tights. She pressed herself further back into the couch, allowing Jasmine to access better purchase as she ground down against denim.

Jasmine wanted all of it right then, immediately, because she'd spent too many years of her life playing it safe, not wanting to get hurt again. She separated from their kiss, burying her face in Leah's neck, and loosening her tie to give her better access. "Upstairs?" she breathed.

Responding with only a nod, Leah picked her up by the thighs, climbing the stairs easily as she unzipped the back of Jasmine's dress. "I meant what I said, you know," she said in a husky voice. "You really do look phenomenal."

"You don't have to suck up, Erickson, you already won," Jasmine replied. Leah set her down on her bedroom rug and she shimmied out of her dress, leaving it in a heap on the floor. She hadn't worn it for very long, but it had done its job. Before she could turn around, Leah was already there, hands all over her, greedy, yearning, and clumsy, fumbling at the waistband of her tights. Jasmine laid back on the bed, letting Leah peel them off and toss them to the floor, discarded.

"I've wanted this from the moment I laid eyes on you," Leah said evenly, kneeling on the bed. "It's why I agreed to your wild scheme in the first place."

"Take off your shirt," Jasmine ordered. "And the jeans." She nestled back onto the pillows, watching as each button was set free from the tyranny of the cotton. "It's not like I haven't seen it before, right?"

Leah huffed out a quiet laugh. "I think this is a little different." She stared as she pulled off her shirt and the tie, dropping them onto the floor. She reached for her belt buckle, and the sound of the metal was almost too much for Jasmine to stand.

"Hurry up," she said.

"Be patient," Leah chastised. "Good things come to those who wait." She pulled off her jeans, crawling up the bed in her matching black sports bra and boxers, the wide elastic band a demure rainbow. She lingered at Jasmine's thighs, staring hungrily as her palms lay against bare skin.

Tired of waiting, and unsure she could stand the delay even one moment longer, Jasmine reached forward, tangling her fingers in Leah's cropped hair, pulling her head down towards where her own thighs met.

Leah breathed through the soft black cotton, the warmth sending an electric jolt through Jasmine's body that held a promising start to the new year. Jasmine groaned, catching Leah's eye and holding her stare, the tension of delayed gratification settling deep in her gut. Jasmine shifted her hips, allowing Leah to remove her underwear, not caring where they wound up.

"You're killing me," she whispered as Leah teased, waited, and tormented, tracing one fingertip through the thicket of dark hair, languishing, taking her time as though they had all the hours in the universe. Jasmine pulled Leah's face to meet her center, and couldn't repress the gasp that escaped her lips as tongue met wet folds, her thoughts already scrambled, already close to the edge. "Wait, wait," she said. "You first."

Leah tilted her head in question, but acquiesced, reversing their positions so that she was the one laid back on pillows staring down at Jasmine. Her muscular thighs were a sight to behold, and it was mere seconds before Jasmine tossed the boxers across the room, where they landed on the doorknob, hanging there.

The movie played downstairs, the muffled sounds drifting up the stairs, the street outside quiet and empty. Jasmine didn't hesitate to bury her face in Leah, needing to bring her to the same level, because she couldn't be the only one needing release like it would kill her if she didn't get it. Leah turned her head to the side, muffling her moans.

"Nuh-uh," Jasmine said, reaching up to take the pillow. "I want to hear you."

"Please," Leah begged, gripping the bars of the headboard with white knuckles. "Please, don't stop."

Jasmine dragged her tongue up and down, teasing at Leah's entrance until she was almost crying out for more contact, and filled the request by circling around the bundle of nerves, sucking gently. Pleased at the response, at how Leah was pressing her hips up off the bed into Jasmine's mouth, she brought her hand up, sliding two fingers in, almost crashing over the edge herself at Leah's cries.

She picked up a slow rhythm, more to tease than to finish, but she had inadvertently unlocked the secret of how Leah worked, because it was less than a minute more before her chest was heaving, her thighs still shaking.

"Can't move," Leah said after a moment, still unable to catch her breath. "You'd better come here."

"This was my plan all along," Jasmine teased, positioning herself over Leah's mouth. She wasn't able to keep her composure for long, unable to keep herself from pressing down against eager tongue, bracing herself against the wall on her forearms, and deeply grateful that they didn't share a wall with neighbors as she let loose a stream of curses and moans, escalating in volume.

Leah lapped at her, probing, charting every ridge, drawing unintelligible characters against her as she worked. Every muscle tensed, Jasmine tipped into the abyss with one final groan, matching Leah's beneath her.

She climbed off, slinking between the sheets and inviting Leah to join her. The feeling of their winded, soft flesh pressed together was enough to set her off again, and perhaps selfishly, she positioned herself against Leah's thigh, rubbing against her until she satisfied herself again.

"Happy New Year," Leah whispered, breaking the silence. "Look, it's snowing."

Jasmine turned over in bed, pulling Leah's arms around her, and watched the snowflakes swirl and drift closer to earth. "I hope it never stops snowing," she said. "I hope we never have to leave this bed."

Leah didn't reply, but tightened her grip around Jasmine's midsection, simultaneously an answer and a quiet promise.

Epilogue

"Mom!" Jasmine shouted from the bottom of the stairs. "Come on, let's go! Whatever is left in there isn't important!" She tapped her foot impatiently, a tote of leftovers in her hands.

"We still have plenty of time," Leah soothed, a box of books tucked under her arm. "It will only take a couple of hours to drive down." She shifted the box to her other arm and laid a hand on the small of Jasmine's back. "The truck is pretty much loaded already."

"Annie!" Martin shouted from the driveway, throwing his arms up in the air. "They aren't going to wait forever, you know!"

"Alright, alright!" Annie relented, jogging down the stairs with something in her hands. "I didn't want you to forget this, Jazzy," she said, placing Damien's snow globe atop the books. "When did he say he'll visit you downstate?"

"As soon as we're settled," Jasmine replied, shooing her out the door. "And thanks. I thought I'd packed it."

Annie snorted an indelicate laugh. "What do you think about that, Leah?" she asked. "A freshly hired archivist who doesn't even know what she packed?"

"No better than a research fellow who can't find her notes," Leah joked. "It's fine. I'm sure they'll turn up as we unpack." She repositioned the snowglobe deeper into the box for safekeeping, wedged between books about the region's geological history and an illustrated analysis of fluorite. "Thank you for offering to drive down with us, I think it would have been frustrating, otherwise."

"I couldn't miss the opportunity to see your new place, could I?" Annie asked, a slight smile pulling at the corners of her lips. "Pictures online never do it justice." She looked past Leah out at her father and shouted, "Right, Dad?"

"Yeah," Martin yelled back. He walked up the driveway again, leaning against the white post on the porch. "You know, if it's terrible, you can both always come back here. Open house. Jazz has the key, that won't change." He took the box from Leah, grunting from the weight. "Leah, you're welcome too, so long as you listen to me ramble on about rocks."

"That's my job, Martin," she replied, taking the box back from him. "Finally." The sun was high in the sky already, offering only a few more hours of unrestricted daylight. "At least it's not as cold as it was last month. Maybe now Jasmine won't freeze in the passenger seat on the way down."

"Says the walking furnace," Jasmine grumbled, but followed it up with a giggle. "I'm just so excited! New beginnings! Adventure!"

"Don't forget to change your forwarding address with Dr. Ahara," Annie urged. "She'll want to keep you as a patient even if you're moving south. And your next appointment—"

Jasmine interrupted her mother with a hug. "I know, Mom," she said evenly. "Don't worry." She checked her watch, frowning. "Don't you have a date tonight? You'll never make it unless we leave five minutes ago."

"Oh, it's just Bruce," Annie replied, trying to hide her blush by pulling her scarf up over her face. "He'll understand if I'm a little late." She zipped up her coat and locked the door, a tear gathering in the corner of her eye. "Oh, I know I'm just being a silly woman," she said, pulling Jasmine and Leah in for a hug. "I just can't bear the thought of you being so far away."

"It's only ninety minutes, Mom," Jasmine soothed. "We'll be back twice a month for dinner, and you can come visit once we have real furniture to sleep on. Given our salaries, that might be a few months."

"Beats Syndicorp," Leah offered. "By a pretty wide margin."

"Low bar," Jasmine joked. "But you're right."

Leah opened the back of the moving truck, setting the box of books inside on the floor. She took a few shirts from her duffel, wrapping the snow globe up before packing it safely in another crate. Everything was stacked high, most of it Jasmine's, and half of that stuff that her mother had bought or insisted they take to their new apartment.

"Hey," Jasmine whispered, coming up behind her to wrap her arms around Leah's waist. "You ready?"

"Yeah," Leah said. "I gave Martin my keys already, and your mom has yours." She leaned back into Jasmine's embrace, staring up at the surprisingly cloudless sky. "I think February has a bad rap," she mused.

"Oh yeah?" Jasmine asked. "Why is that?"

"Because from where I'm standing, it looks like a pretty hopeful future." Leah turned, planting a kiss on Jasmine's lips. "And I'm excited to discover it with you."

* * *

About the Author

Ryann Fletcher is a writer who lives impostor syndrome and too many craft supplies. She writes sapphic science fiction and fantasy, and likes to cook.

You can connect with me on:

- https://ryannfletcher.com
- https://facebook.com/RyannFletcherWrites
- https://instagram.com/RyannFletcherWrites
- https://www.tiktok.com/@ryannfletcherwrites
- https://patreon.com/RyannFletcherWrites

Subscribe to my newsletter:

- https://campsite.bio/ryannfletcherwrites

Also by Ryann Fletcher

Deus Ex Mechanic

Alice is the best mechanic in the corrupt coalition regime, and enjoys her quiet life. When she's taken by one of the most infamous pirate crews in the near systems, everything is thrown into chaos, and it's not long before hard questions arise about where she stands in the fight against injustice, and her growing attraction towards a certain crew member.

Violet is the captain of the pirate ship, the Cricket, and damn proud of her reputation. When she reluctantly kidnaps a brilliant mechanic, things start to spin wildly out of her control, secrets get spilled, and she has to make the tough decision on whether to follow her growing feelings for a coalition employee, or put her crew first.

Will the pirates prevail, or will they be destroyed by the Coalition... or rival pirates?